PRAISE FOR *Cold Blood, Hot Sea*
(Foreword INDIES 2016 Finalist)

Sleuths will have to figure out who's done it, but the real crime is the backdrop here: the endless heating of a fragile planet.

—BILL McKIBBEN, author of *Eaarth*

PRAISE FOR *Demon Spirit, Devil Sea*
(IPPY Award Winner)

Another great read…D'Avanzo writes compelling novels that take you to wonderful oceanside places where terrible things happen.

—GEORGE SMITH, outdoors writer for the *Bangor Daily News*

PRAISE FOR *Secrets Haunt the Lobsters' Sea*
(Foreword INDIES Mystery Finalist,
IPPY Fiction Silver Winner)

Charlene D'Avanzo is a natural storyteller and a passionate scientist, and she brings both aspects of herself to her third novel, Secrets Haunt the Lobsters' Sea.

—PAUL DOIRON, author of the Mike Bowditch crime novels

PRAISE FOR *Glass Eels, Shattered Sea*
(IPPY Fiction Bronze Winner)

Readers understand that glass eel trafficking is an international tragedy.

—KIM MILLICK, author of the *Rookie Warden*

THE SHARK, THE GIRL & THE SEA

Charlene D'Avanzo

A MARA TUSCONI MYSTERY

The Shark, the Girl & the Sea
Copyright © 2021 Charlene D'Avanzo

ISBN: 978-1-63381-287-1

All rights reserved. No part of this book may be reproduced in any form or by any electronic or mechanical means, including information storage and retrieval systems, without permission in writing from the author, except by a reviewer, who may quote brief passages in review.

This is a work of fiction. Names, characters, places, and incidents either are the product of the author's imagination or are used fictitiously, and any resemblance to actual persons, living or dead, is coincidental.

Front cover design by:
Rick Whipple, Sky Island Studio

Designed and produced by:
Maine Authors Publishing
12 High Street, Thomaston, Maine
www.maineauthorspublishing.com

Printed in the United States of America

This series is dedicated to scientists struggling to understand the extraordinarily complex phenomena associated with climate change.

AUTHOR'S NOTE

IN THIS NOVEL I REFER TO OCEANOGRAPHIC AND SHARK studies, plus climate change research more generally. I attempt to represent the science as accurately as possible in a fictional story. Readers will find additional information plus references on my website (charlenedavanzo.com).

THE SHARK, THE GIRL & THE SEA

1

My office on the Maine Oceanographic Institute's uppermost floor offers a killer view of Spruce Harbor. In need of a bracer, I pushed away from my desk, stretched, and walked over to the window to scan the scene below.

Beyond MOI's docks, the usual array of marine craft pulled on their moorings in the afternoon breeze—five lobster boats enjoyed their Labor Day reprise alongside a sailboat, plus a couple of dinghies that waited for their owners' return. None of it foretold a hint of disaster in the offing.

My growling stomach demanded attention, so I grabbed the lunch bag I'd packed that morning, locked the office door, and hurried down two sets of stairs to the second floor and Harvey's chemistry lab.

Harvey, baptized Harville, is my dearest friend and confidante, and a gifted marine chemist. She'd recently stepped in as MOI Biology Department chair and somehow managed those duties and her research at the same time. Truly a wonder woman.

Harvey's office door was locked, so I tried her lab. She was clearly busy and out of earshot in the glassed-in instrument analysis room she'd dubbed "the cell." A woman I didn't know sat at one of the lab tables and flipped through what looked like a manual of some sort.

I walked over to the table. "Hi, there."

Blinking, she looked up, pushed dirty-blond bangs aside, and grinned. "Gosh, I didn't hear you come in."

I returned her smile. "Gripping book, is it?"

She missed my cynicism entirely. "Sure. *Marine Chemists' Analytical Methods*. It's the bible, you know."

"Actually," I said, "I'm an ecologist and not a chemist, so you've educated me." I held out my hand and added, "Mara Tusconi."

She stood and pumped my arm. "Wow! It's an honor to meet you, Dr. Tusconi. I'm Caroline McBride and, I dearly hope, Dr. Allison's next grad student. Please call me Cary."

Cary and I turned as Harvey stuck her head out of the analysis room. "Mara, hi. I see you've met Caroline. Do you have time to show her around? This pesky instrument isn't behaving, so I'll be tied up for a while."

"Sure," I said. "You need something to eat, so I'll leave you my sandwich and take Caroline—Cary—over to the Neap Tide for lunch."

Harvey nodded. "Excellent. Um, Cary, I'll surely be done here this afternoon, and we can chat then." The door swooshed as she pulled it closed and faced the irksome instrument once more.

As we walked through the village of Spruce Harbor, Cary bubbled with enthusiasm. "It's incredible to be here. I've wanted to be an oceanographer as long as I can remember."

"Are you from Maine?" I asked.

"Sure am. Lived in Birch Cove Blight near Phippsburg all my life and spent a lot of it on, in, and under the water. My mom thinks I'm a reincarnated seal."

The image gave me a chuckle at the time, but looking back, it was uncannily tragic.

I carried our tray of sandwiches, chips, and drinks to a relatively quiet spot in the back corner as the hopeful graduate student trailed behind and took in Neap Tide's distinct clientele. Swarthy deckhands from MOI ships traded insults and jokes from their respective tables alongside bookish types who, oblivious to the cacophony around them, leaned over newspapers and research magazines.

Seated at our table, Cary bubbled over. "This is *so* cool. The people who do oceanographic research are all right here."

Nodding, I agreed. "Sure. Scientists, obviously, but those seamen make it happen. They take us hundreds of miles offshore and help us deploy unwieldy, expensive instruments from the pitching aft deck of a ship. Sometimes I think they don't get enough credit." I finished my chicken-salad sandwich, downed my Diet Coke, and asked, "When did you decide to study marine science?"

"Actually," she said, "I can't remember when I *didn't* want to be an oceanographer. I've always liked science, plus living on the ocean, you know. It just made sense to make that my career. Was that how it was for you too?"

"Partly," I said. "My parents were marine scientists, so I decided to follow their example."

Cary raised her eyebrows. "Gosh. So where are they now?"

I looked to the side. "They died in a research submarine accident." Anticipating the young woman's disquiet, I added, "That was quite a while ago, but it's a reminder that oceanographic research can be dangerous." I glanced at my watch. "And speaking of dangerous, a scientist who studies sharks, Brady MacFarlane, will talk about his research in twenty minutes. I'm going, so would you like to join me?"

Already on her feet, Cary grabbed her tray. "Are you kidding? That sounds fantastic."

MOI's auditorium was already half full when we walked down a side aisle and found seats near the front. I was wiggling out of my jacket when Ted, my colleague and partner, took the seat next to mine.

Free of the coat, I combed fingers through my hair, introduced Ted to Cary, and settled back as Frederick Dixon walked onto the stage.

2

DIXON INTRODUCED HIMSELF AS THE MOI DIRECTOR and said, "I'm delighted to welcome all of you, researchers, crew, visitors, and Spruce Harbor locals. For some, scientist Brady MacFarlane needs no introduction since you've seen him on the popular *Shark Science* TV show. As a great white shark expert from Scripps Institution of Oceanography in California, Brady's goal is to help people understand that these animals are not the monsters we see in popular films. In fact, sharks have much more to fear from us than we do from them." Smiling, Dixon turned and extended his hand to the man walking up the stairs to the stage. "Please, everyone, welcome Dr. MacFarlane to MOI."

MacFarlane strode quickly across the stage, and from his physique, I pegged him as a runner, scuba diver, or both. The audience had quieted by the time he reached the podium.

"Thank you, Dr. Dixon. Believe it or not, this is my first visit to Maine Oceanographic, and I am absolutely delighted to be here. For the last decade or so I have dedicated myself to debunking the many misconceptions people have about great white sharks and replacing those myths with what we know and don't know about shark behavior, biology, and their very uncertain future."

Perhaps to put some in the audience at ease, MacFarlane began with some humor about how great whites are usually depicted. "It's truly unfortunate that these remarkable animals are usually only shown during the brief, albeit stunning, moment when they are eating. Imagine if someone made a movie about people and started with a scene from Thanksgiving dinner. You'd see father vigorously sawing off the turkey leg and handing it to his son. The young man would eagerly reach for the appendage, bite into the meat with his pearly white teeth, vigorously chew, swallow, and return for another bite. Except for lip-smacking and occasional 'thanks,' the room would be quiet as everyone around the table repeated the process of mastication and ingestion. I'm sure you get my point."

Projecting his computer onto a large screen, MacFarlane began his formal presentation with the most common misconceptions about sharks. "While sharks are enormously powerful creatures," he said, "you are more likely to be killed by your kitchen toaster than a shark. Another thing most people don't realize is how sharks have helped people over the years. For instance, until 1947, shark-liver oil was the main source of vitamin A for folks who needed it. Shark cartilage has been used as an artificial skin for burn victims during the healing process, and shark corneas have been transplanted into people's eyes." MacFarlane paused for a moment, scanned the room, and added, "It's very sad that our obsession with a single aspect of shark biology—that they are carnivores—overshadows all the rest, including knowledge about how sharks navigate and communicate, shark sex, their life history, and so much more."

Over the next hour, MacFarlane limited his presentation to intriguing, poorly understood white shark behaviors. That included the "tail snap," a behavior in which the shark lifted its caudal fin out of the water, paused for a moment, then forcefully slapped the fin on the water surface. He described various interpretations of this behavior, including that it was a social display for other sharks, a threat, or something altogether different, such as some kind of displacement activity. MacFarlane's next slide listed what he called "surprising shark facts," such as: 1) sharks are excellent mothers who may have a litter only every other year with one or two pups, 2) a shark's lateral line picks up vibrations in the water created by approaching fish or another shark, and 3) in a maneuver called "bite and spit," sharks usually release their victim and wait for it to bleed to death and stop moving, which is why humans often survive such attacks.

The time went quickly, and I was surprised when MacFarlane showed his last slide, glanced at his watch, and said he had time to answer only one question.

A crewmember standing in the back asked a critical one. "I understand that scientists are tagging sharks off Massachusetts. By water, that's not far from the coast of Maine. Many of us here spend time on and even in the ocean, so do we need to be on the lookout for sharks?"

Nodding, MacFarlane said, "That's a really important point I was going to address if nobody brought it up. The short answer is yes, we see sharks off Cape Cod near Provincetown and the National Seashore south of there. And straight shot, a shark could make it from P-town to Portland in half a day. In addition, great whites feed on marine mammals such as seals, which, as you know, are pretty common along the Maine coast. Sharks hunt during the day, when their prey are active. Unfortunately, that's when people are in the water as well. However, it's important to emphasize that shark attacks on humans are extremely rare. Worldwide last year, ten people were killed by sharks, all in Australia. So statistically, you are much more likely to die in a car accident on your way to work."

The auditorium was quiet for a moment as we all took in this vital information. Then MacFarlane answered one more question, an odd one, I thought.

A guy in the back whose voice I didn't recognize asked, "If someone wanted to attract a shark, what's the best way to do it?"

MacFarlane tried for a little humor. "Well, I wouldn't suggest you try this at home, but fish oil is a pretty good shark attractant." And with that, he left the stage to appreciative applause.

The place was packed, so it was a while before we could file out. As we reached the lobby, I asked Ted which part of the talk most interested him.

"The list of our misconceptions gets your attention," Ted said, "but MacFarlane's focus on the tail snap research helped me appreciate how hard it is to do behavior studies on these animals. Everything about it—all the logistics, never mind the danger—you have to be really driven to do it. I'll stick to boring old plankton research any day."

By that time Harvey had made her way over to us. Before she and Cary left to find a quiet spot to talk, I asked Harvey if Connor, her live-in partner, needed a reminder about the barbecue party at my house the following afternoon.

Laughing, she said, "Are you kidding? Connor pulled out all my cookbooks to find the perfect way to charcoal grill lobster and was heading out to the lobster pound as I left the house."

I grinned. "Well, you know what I say about people who like to eat."

In harmony, she and I said, "People who like to eat together are the best people to be with."

"And Cary," I added, "why don't you join the party as well? It'd be a great way to meet some of the MOI scientists and students. Harvey can give you directions. Hope you can make it."

"Gosh, really?" she said. "That'd be just fantastic. Thanks so very much!"

3

THE FOLLOWING AFTERNOON WAS A SATURDAY, AND coastal Maine lived up to its "Vacationland" moniker. There was nary a cloud in the sky, afternoon temperatures peaked in the low seventies, and a light wind ruffled the sea surface. My house, which overlooks the ocean, offered views of sailboats in the distance as well as activity on the beach below. From the deck, I was watching several of the scientists' children splash each other in the chilly water when Harvey walked over.

"Well, Mara," she said, "you sure won the weather lottery— perfect day for everyone to just hang out together." Squinting, she shaded her eyes with one hand and scanned the water. "My goodness. Someone's out there pretty far, and whoever it is must be a pretty strong swimmer."

I'd been watching a group of eider ducks from the deck earlier that morning, and my field glasses were still on the picnic table. I reached for the binocs, raised them to my eyes, adjusted the optics, and scanned the water. Sure enough, somebody was swimming a hundred yards or so off the beach. When the swimmer turned toward me to take a breath, I could tell who it was.

I handed the binoculars to Harvey. "Take a look. I'm pretty sure it's Cary."

Harvey fixed the field glasses on the same general location for a half-minute, then handed them back. "Yup. That's her. Wow, she *is* a strong swimmer."

"Cary lives near Popham Beach," I said. "She told me she swims off the rocks there all summer."

Harvey raised her eyebrows. "That water's really cold. She probably wears a wetsuit, but still, the girl's got stamina. Um, sorry to take off, but there's a clutch of chemists down below I should join. And Connor is probably on the beach grilling lobster by now. You'll want to see how he does it."

Harvey took off to join her "clutch" of MOI colleagues, so I decided to check on Ted, who had taken charge of my gas grill at the far end of the deck. He was cooking usual barbeque fare—hamburgers and hot dogs—and from the depleted quantity of both it appeared that he'd been pretty busy.

As I approached, he was on his cell phone. Eyeing me, he quickly ended the call.

"Anything important?" I asked.

"What? Oh, the call. Nah, just some Woods Hole stuff."

"Right," I said. "Um, appears as if we've got a hungry crowd."

He nodded. "Yeah. I'm sending anyone interested to Connor down on the beach for lobster."

I nodded. "My next stop. After that, I can take over for you if you want."

Saying, "I'm good," he returned to his culinary duties. At the top of the path that led down to the cobble beach I turned to look up at the deck. Laughing, Ted was on the phone again.

Reaching the beach, I realized I'd lived in Maine all my life but had never grilled the state's beloved crustacean. By the size of the crowd gathered around Connor down the cobble a bit, it looked like I wasn't alone.

Irish to the core with curly black hair, a heavy Maine accent, and a heart of gold, Connor Doyle loved entertaining a crowd. The onlookers who watched his every move confirmed that Connor was in his element. Listening to him as I approached, I could understand why.

"First," he said, "use sharp kitchen shears like these to make a shallow cut down the top of each tail." He leaned over to execute the cut before replacing the shears with a hefty kitchen knife. "Next, put a good-sized knife into the mark you just made and cut straight down through the lobster flesh. Stop when you hit the bottom shell."

Leaning over Connor and the lobster, the group watched him execute each step.

"Finally," he said, "I'll flatten out the cut lobster tail with my hands to expose the meat so I can spread softened butter all over it."

Connor carried his cut-and-buttered lobster to a smoking coal fire closer to the water as his culinary gaggle followed behind. I was about to join them when a woman behind me called out my name. I turned to see Cary ringing out her dripping hair.

I reached her and squeezed her hand. "My god, you are frozen. Use the bathroom off the kitchen if you'd like a hot shower, and help yourself to a clean towel."

Rolling her shoulders, she said, "H-have to admit, I am pretty cold. My wetsuit usually keeps me pretty warm, but I didn't bring it."

"Then off with you," I said. "Grab your clothes, hop in the shower, and you'll be good as new in a couple of minutes."

By seven-thirty the last guests had left, and Harvey, Connor, Ted, and I sat on the deck to watch a reddening horizon that promised a stellar sunset.

"I'm happy the get-together came off as well as it did," I said. "And Connor, you and your lobster stole the show down on the beach."

He grinned. "Me and my lobster. I like that. Hey, you might be interested in something a guy in the group described. He called it a lost herring industry that used to be up in Lubec just south of the Canadian border. Said there're old smokehouses on a pier where the floorboards and timbers still hold the char and smell from decades of smoke. I'd really like to check that out."

"Sounds like a field trip," I said. "I think the party went pretty well, but it's nice to just chill with you guys."

"It *was* a great party," Harvey said. "I especially enjoyed talking to Brady MacFarlane, although some of what he told me about sharks in New England waters was worrisome."

That got my attention. "What do you mean?"

She shrugged. "There are a couple of things I wish he'd mentioned during his talk. But maybe he didn't want to scare people."

I stared at her. "*Things*? What things?"

"Reports about seals with bite marks north of here. That's not unusual, he said, but the number—ten—is pretty high. Besides that, a seal carcass was found washed up on an island off Phippsburg with a twenty-inch bite wound."

The four of us were silent as the new information sank in.

"Mara," Ted said, "you kayak up that way, don't you? Maybe you shouldn't."

"To a shark, seals and kayaks couldn't be more different," I said. "Sharks have good eyesight and are on the lookout for seals, which are dark gray. Besides that, MacFarlane said they could detect low-frequency sounds like blood pumping through a seal's body. My kayak's hull is white and, of course, there's no heart that pumps blood. Unless I fall out of my boat, which has never happened, I'm okay. As MacFarlane said, there's more danger in my drive up to Phippsburg than the kayak trip itself."

"But someone in your group might end up in the water," Harvey added.

"Well, sure," I agreed. "But that's extremely unlikely."

4

THAT NIGHT, AS TED AND I LAY IN BED TALKING, HE SAID, "I really don't like the idea of you paddling around Phippsburg."

"The thing is," I countered, "a couple of my kayak buddies and I planned this paddle last year. They are summer people and leave next week, so this is it. Maine Marine Patrol posts shark alerts, which I'll keep checking until I leave in the morning. At this point, there's nothing about sharks or evidence of shark attacks on their site."

"It's up to you," he said. "But I still don't like it."

After breakfast, I filled the back of my Subaru wagon with my kayak gear. That's a lot of stuff—two paddles (one for backup), spray skirt, life jacket, wetsuit, waterproof paddle jacket, neoprene boots and gloves, paddle float, kayak cart, lunch in a waterproof container, two bottles of water, extra clothes in a waterproof bag, chart, and a weather radio. Before he'd left, Ted had helped me tie the seventeen-foot-long kayak to the racks on the rooftop.

It was another lovely late summer day, and the weather channel folks predicted low-to-moderate wind, no heavy chop, and plenty of sun. At the put-in, my friends Sarah and Maureen helped me unload my kayak and carry it down to the water. Naturally, I returned the favor. It took me fifteen-odd minutes to stuff backup kayak gear—emergency dry clothes, food, extra water, and my weather radio—into the dry hatches. Each of us secured a waterproof chart within view on the deck in front of our cockpit, slid into our respective boat, grabbed our paddle, and pushed off. After all the preparation, we could finally relish the pleasure of being on Maine's pristine salt water together.

Back on shore, we'd already picked our route—south following Phippsburg's rocky ledges until we reached a good stopping place to rest and have lunch. We'd take it from there after that. Since there was a pretty good swell, we had to be careful to avoid backwash from waves crashing off the rocks. On the other hand, given the sea state, we also didn't want to drift out very far.

We'd only paddled for ten minutes when Maureen spotted a good-sized black-and-white bird a couple hundred yards ahead.

"Loon," she announced. "Big one too. Sorry, but I gotta get some pics of that guy."

Sliding to a stop, Maureen stowed her paddles across the cockpit, lifted the waterproof camera hanging from her neck, and snapped a couple of photos while Sarah and I waited behind her. I was about to ask Sarah about a fish-oil smell when the loon dove and disappeared beneath the surface as a red kayak rounded a ledge and headed toward us.

Maureen mumbled an expletive and slipped the camera back into its waterproof pouch.

The red kayak came to a sliding stop to our starboard as the paddler introduced himself. "Nice day for a kayak trip, ladies. Name's Luke O'Sullivan, and I live yon in that house back there. Paddled here before?"

I figured the huge house overlooking the rocks behind the guy was "yon," that we were supposed to be impressed, and that Luke wanted to impress us further with his paddling wisdom.

Looking out to sea, I said, "Thanks, Luke, but we've kayaked here before, so we're good." I added, "Have a nice day," as we paddled past the open-mouthed man and continued on our way.

The remainder of our trip continued to be a sea kayaker's delight. Bright sunlight reflecting off the water was warm, so during the first rest stop we traded our heavyweight paddling jackets for lighter ones and reapplied sunscreen to our faces.

Hours later, my cheery mood darkened a bit as we glided past Luke's house and approached the take-out. "Look at that thing," I said. "It's enormous. I can't imagine he lives there alone, but you never know."

It was pushing six p.m. when we'd secured the kayaks onto roof racks, stowed wet gear into our respective cars, and said our goodbyes. During the summer, I avoided driving busy Route 1 in the dark, but I knew there'd still be plenty of light for the trip home. In the fall this far north, the sun wouldn't set for another couple of hours. Of course, Mainers paid for that advantage during the snowy months, when sunset arrived in the middle of the afternoon.

Back home over dinner, Ted surprised me after I enthused about the paddle. "The few times you and I kayaked together, we've left from here," he said. "I've never seen Phippsburg's rocky coastline, and it does sound pretty spectacular. Tomorrow's the last day of our long weekend, so why don't we paddle there?"

I squeezed his hand. "Really? I'd love that. But we'll have to leave really early to avoid Route 1 traffic, and it might be pretty bad on the way back."

"Not a problem," he said. "I know a back road that'll get us home traffic-free."

And that's why I unexpectedly returned to the Phippsburg put-in for the second day in a row. Sea kayakers do often paddle the same routes because, well, things are never really the same. Wind speed and direction, weather, sea state, water temperature, and the like change from day to day, especially in "if you don't like the weather wait a minute" New England.

For a little variety, Ted and I headed north for the first half of our paddle and reversed course after lunch. Four hours, a lunch stop, and a shared-granola bar on the water later, Ted and I floated off the put-in.

"Ready to head home?" he asked.

I shaded my eyes and looked out to sea. "The wind's come up, and the waves are breaking. So yeah."

Pointing at Luke's mansion, Ted said, "That house is huge and looks like it belongs in Hollywood."

I was about to tell him about the mansion's owner when a splash in the water dead ahead caught Ted's eye. "Mara, look. There's someone swimming off the ledge near the mansion. I sure hope they know what they're doing."

"I bet that's Cary," I said. "Remember Harvey's new grad student? She lives around here and told me she swims off these rocks all the time. Let's get closer to see if that's her."

We quick-paddled and were within shouting distance when it happened. One moment the swimmer was doing a crawl stoke with a strong, steady rhythm and the next they'd disappeared beneath the water, come up thrashing and shrieking, and gone down again. In the lead, I stopped paddling and glided to a stop about twenty yards from where the swimmer went under. Frozen in horror, I stared at the spreading red stain that marked the spot.

It was Ted's yell—"She's coming back up! Let's get her out of the water!"—that snapped me into action.

When Cary surfaced, I couldn't tell if she was conscious. Her wetsuit helped her float, and Ted somehow managed to drag her over to my boat and drape her limp body across my bow. Ted pulled out his phone and called 911 while I stroked gently toward the launch site. We'd just reached our destination when the welcome scream of sirens echoed in the distance.

Tears wet my cheeks as I spoke to the unconscious young woman lying across my deck. "Cary, please, please stay with us. Help is on the way. They'll take good care of you. I promise they will."

5

TWO MEDICS JUMPED OUT OF THEIR VEHICLE, RAN ACROSS the cobble, and waded into the water as I glided toward them. One stopped my forward momentum as the other looked at Cary and barked, "What happened?"

"Shark attack, we think. She was swimming off the rocks."

Eyebrows furrowed, he glanced up at me, scanned Cary's bleeding legs and chest, repeated "shark attack," and added, "good Christ."

What happened next remains pretty much a blur. I recall a couple of guys carrying Cary on a canvas stretcher off the beach and up to an ambulance. Two policemen took separate statements from me and Ted. One draped a blanket across my shoulders when I started shivering uncontrollably. Twice I asked the officer who spoke to me—Lieutenant Bradbury—about Cary's prospects, and each time he shook his head and said he didn't know.

Interviews finished and contact information collected, Bradbury shook our hands and thanked Ted and me. "You folks good to head on home?"

"Lieutenant, we're okay," I said. "It's Cary who's going through hell right now. To find out how she is, do we call the hospital or what?"

He handed me his card. "Since you aren't family, I don't know what they'll tell you. Here's my information. Contact me tomorrow, and I'll let you know what I can."

After I thanked Bradbury, he gave me a quick nod and headed back to his cruiser. Silent, Ted and I stood on the windy beach and watched the vehicle until it was out of sight.

I barely recall the ride from Phippsburg back to Spruce Harbor. Guessing I was in no shape to navigate, Ted took the keys and drove instead. While I remember him saying we'd done what we could, I'm not sure what my response was, and I cried off and on during the trip. Back home after we unloaded the boats, I decided to take a hot bath. Warm and dry, I padded into the bedroom, pulled on pajamas, climbed into bed, and didn't wake again until morning.

But when I did, I called out, "Fish oil, Ted. Fish oil!"

Rolling over to face me, Ted mumbled, "Wha?"

Sitting up, I said, "Yesterday, on the paddle with Sarah and Maureen, I smelled fish oil. I'm sure I did."

Blinking, he repeated, "Fish oil?"

"Don't you remember? Someone asked MacFarlane how to attract sharks, and he said you could use fish oil."

He yawned. "Mara, maybe it's because I just woke up, but I'm not with you."

"How to prove it, I have no idea, but I think somebody poured fish oil as a shark lure into the water where Caroline swam every day."

Seated in the kitchen after three cups of coffee apiece we sorted though the implications of my outrageous claim. First, if I was right, what happened to Caroline was intentional and not an accident. This meant, second, that someone, assuming they were sane, believed they had a very good reason to harm her. Further, this person had knowledge and opportunity—how to carry out such a bizarre incident plus ability to pull it off.

"Well," Ted said. "That does narrow it down."

I frowned. "What do you mean?"

"If what happened was intentional, whoever did it is very likely local. Otherwise, unless they were very lucky, someone who lives there could've noticed a stranger putting fish oil in the water and probably smelled it too. That's a big risk to take."

"I suppose they could've done it at night," I said.

Ted shook his head. "I don't think so. The smell would've been gone by the time anyone was on or in the water."

"What if the attractant isn't an oil but something like dead fish under the water in a weighted a mesh bag? Or maybe in a trap of some sort? You could put that out and leave it for days."

Ted nodded. "True. But, again, unless they are local they'd risk attracting attention. By now, all the locals know what happened, and anyone suspecting anything would've contacted the police."

"Hmm," I said.

"Hmm, what?"

"When I kayaked with Sarah and Maureen, we met a pretty obnoxious guy named Luke. He made sure we knew that mansion overlooking the water was his and tried telling us where to paddle until I let him know we weren't interested."

With a shrug, Ted said, "To point out the obvious, because a guy is unpleasant doesn't mean he's a killer."

"Sure," I said. "But how am I going to find out?"

Standing, Ted said, "I've got to get going. Oh, and Mara, you *aren't* going to find out."

Ted's proclamation notwithstanding, over the next day, I devoted my spare mental resources to how I could find out if, why, and by what means Luke had harmed Cary. In the end, I came to the following conclusions: 1) I might find clues to what happened to Cary in Luke's house somewhere, 2) to do that I needed to make Luke believe I actually liked him, and

3) the one guy who knew absolutely every local—Harvey's partner Connor—could probably help me pull off that ruse.

When the weather was good, Harvey and I often enjoyed our bag lunches behind the science building seated on a little swath of grass next to the water. Legs dangling over a ledge, we watched waves splash against pilings as we shared whatever was foremost on our mind. On this day that, naturally, was Cary.

Harvey pulled a sandwich out of her bag. "Any word about how she's doing?"

"No," I said, "and that's frustrating. I called Lieutenant Bradbury this morning, but he hasn't gotten back to me. I'll try again when I get back to my office."

"And something else is on your mind, right?"

"Yup, which is why I'll never try to hide anything from you, Harvey. It's a plan I'd like to run by you."

She unwrapped the sandwich. "Sure thing, girlfriend. I'll eat while you talk."

6

HARVEY MUNCHED, AND I OUTLINED MY PLAN AND ITS justification.

"First," I said, "I just don't think the attack was an accident, and if I'm right the culprit had to be a local with easy access to the water right there. The guy I'm wondering about, Luke, lives in a mansion within view of where Cary was swimming."

"And you wonder about him because…?"

"At this point, it's only a hunch. He was kind of obnoxious when I met him on the water with Maureen and Sarah, but that doesn't mean much, of course. So mostly it's that he lives right near where the fish oil smell was so strong."

She took a bite, swallowed, and said, "Fish oil?"

"Yeah. I'm thinking somebody might've poured fish oil into the water where Caroline always swam."

"Oh right," Harvey said. "MacFarlane said fish oil is a powerful shark lure." She scrunched up her nose like she does when something doesn't make sense.

"What?" I asked.

She shrugged. "The big question."

"Why in the world would Luke want to harm Cary?"

"Yup," she agreed. "And I'm guessing you think Connor can help you with that."

I shrugged. "He's a native Mainer plus a retired cop who seems to know something about nearly everyone. Besides that, Connor is Irish and given his name, Luke O'Sullivan must be

Irish as well. I'm guessing Irish gossip gets around pretty fast in our state."

Standing, she said, "Mara, Connor will help anyway he can; you know that. I've got to get back to the lab now, but if you come over tonight the two of you can cook up a plan while I cook dinner."

I got to my feet as well. "Perfect. Ted's on his way down to Woods Hole, and I'd much rather be with you guys than home alone fretting about what's happened."

Standing beside the garden, I was enjoying the fragrance of Harvey's roses when Connor opened the kitchen door and stepped onto the deck. He held up a glass of white wine. "Come on up, Mara. Here's your whatever-you-call-it fancy Italian wine."

I slid into an LL Bean Adirondack chair, accepted the glass, and took a sip. "Lovely. It's called Gavi and is Angelo's favorite summer wine."

Connor settled onto the picnic table's wooden bench, reached for his can of beer, took a slug, and smacked his lips. "Now *that's* a real summer brew. And speaking of Angelo, since he took up with that Angelina, he's lost interest in fishing. I've been goin' alone."

My stomach tightened at the mention of Angelo's lover. My godfather, who had selflessly assumed the role of parent when my parents died, absolutely deserved a companion and confidante. My jealousy was unfair, and I was struggling to deal with it.

"To tell you the truth," I said, "I haven't seen much of him myself."

While Connor's quick nod told me he understood, he was kind enough to let it go.

"Right, then, Mara. Um, before I give you the straight skinny on this Luke O'Sullivan I need to know why you care about the man."

So, once more, I described my brief interaction with O'Sullivan and hunch that Cary's encounter with a shark was no accident.

Nodding as I spoke, Connor listened carefully to my account. I ended with, "Of course, it's just intuition. I have no proof."

He swallowed another slug of beer and said, "Well, you know what the Irish say about intuition."

Grinning, I waited for the answer.

"The Gaelic basically translates as, 'We just know and that's that.'"

"So, you think I may be onto something?" I asked.

"Maybe you can decide after I tell you what I know about Luke O'Sullivan."

I settled back into the oversized wooden chair, sipped wine, and got an earful.

"Around 1850 or so, over a million starving Irish left their homeland and sailed to the United States. The ones who came up here mainly went to industrial cities like Bangor, Augusta, and Portland. Some opened pubs and the like, others became musicians, still others priests. The O'Sullivans were well-known politicians happy to do favors for a price—certain favors cost more money, if you get my meaning."

"So," I said, "Luke O'Sullivan comes from tainted money."

"He does," Connor agreed. "I wish I could say it's all history."

"But you can't," I added.

He shook his head. "No. The details are confidential, but I'll give you the upshot. Luke O'Sullivan is bad news."

1

"**B**AD NEWS AS IN WATCH MY BUTT, OR BAD NEWS AS IN criminal?" I asked.

Connor shrugged. "Whether there's crime I don't know for sure. But certainly you should keep an eye out."

Thinking for a moment, I swirled what was left of my wine. "Well, that does complicate things. I was hoping to, you know, become friends and maybe visit him in his house."

Connor raised an eyebrow. "And then what?"

"To be honest, I hadn't gotten further than that. The gold mine would be evidence that he knows how to attract sharks, but that's not the kind of thing you'd leave lying around your house."

Connor finished his beer and put the glass on the table. "We've been talking about means, Mara. Important, of course, but you are missing something critical."

"Motivation."

He nodded. "Yes indeed. At this point, the only obvious connection between Luke and Cary is location. They lived near each other. So they might know each other, but that's all."

I let that sink in for a minute and added, "You're right. I need more information to move forward. The thing is I don't know Luke O'Sullivan or even anyone who does."

Connor reached over and squeezed my hand. "Harvey's probably wondering where we are. I know a lot of folks, so give me a little time to poke around and get back to you."

Connor's "a little time" was quite a bit less than I expected. At six-thirty the following morning I was still working on my first cup of coffee when the kitchen phone rang. Expecting Ted, I picked it up and was startled by Connor's voice.

"You aren't gonna believe this."

"Ah, good morning to you as well," I said.

Missing or ignoring my sarcasm, he added, "Meet me at the Lee Side after work around five," and hung up.

During the day I holed up in my office, where there was plenty on my computer's desktop demanding attention. Unfortunately, I didn't make much progress reviewing grant proposals and research papers because I found myself wondering what I wasn't "gonna believe." Was Luke O'Sullivan a criminal of some kind or something altogether different?

Finally, it was time to walk over to the Lee Side restaurant and bar to meet Connor. Predictably, Joey, the Lee Side's longtime owner, was polishing the long slab of oak that served as his bar. And also as usual, Joey treated me like a regular even though I hadn't been there for months.

"Hi there, Mara. White wine?"

"Perfect," I said. "I'm meeting Connor Doyle. Is he here yet?"

Joey glanced over at the door. "He's walkin' in now. Take a booth, both of you, and I'll bring Connor's favorite brew right over."

I sipped my wine while Connor finished a beer and ordered another before he was ready to, as he put it, "get down to brass tacks."

"Let me guess," I said. "Luke has served time."

Connor shook his head. "Not even close. The guy's got a reputation, but it's for misplaced suspicion."

"He's paranoid?"

"Delusional, emotionally unstable, psychotic."

"Has he done anything dangerous?"

"Nothing that's been reported."

Thinking, I swirled the remaining wine at the bottom of my glass. "I suppose it's possible Luke is convinced Cary harmed his family or something like that. You know, an awful act of some sort that she didn't commit. The problem is that there's no way we can find out."

Chuckling, Connor said, "If she's still alive, there's a genuine Saint Mary Mead-type sleuth in Phippsburg. Bet she could help us out."

With a grin, I asked, "A Miss Marple?"

"Close. Her name is Malissie Martin."

"Malissie Martin?" I repeated. "Seriously?"

"Yes, indeed," he said. "Martin is a common last name in the state, but she's the only Malissie I've ever met. You are gonna love her. I know you will. And be sure to call her Ms. and not Miss."

And that is why the very next day Connor and I were seated in a Victorian-style "drawing room" sipping tea with Ms. Malissie Martin, an "older" woman with white hair and sharp blue eyes that missed little.

Carefully placing my china cup on the tea tray, I said, "Thank you, Ms. Martin, for seeing us on such short notice."

"Not at all, my dear, not at all. What happened to poor Caroline was just dreadful, of course. I've known her family for the longest time. She was a lovely girl. And please call me Malissie."

"Malissie," I repeated. "How about Luke O'Sullivan? Have you known his family for a long time too?"

"The O'Sullivans have owned property in Phippsburg for generations. Good, solid family. Once in a while, of course, a problem child like Luke O'Sullivan comes along."

"And Luke's a problem because…"

"Funny thing, that. Even as a child Luke was convinced other kids had it better than he did—faster bike, fancier TV, you name it—even though they didn't. It was sad, really."

"So he was paranoid," I said.

She nodded. "Back then, they called it mistrustful, but paranoid is the same thing. 'Course the boy had a reason to be miserable with what happened to mother and his older sister."

That got my attention. "His mother and sister?"

"They died in a car accident, must be five years ago now. Hit and run. A female was driving, but they never identified who it was."

8

Reviewing what we'd learned from Malissie as Connor drove the "back way" home, it was a good half hour before it dawned on me that the countryside we'd passed through was totally unfamiliar.

"Um, Connor, where the heck are we?"

"A special place in Maine I'd bet you've never seen is down this way just a tad more."

About to protest that surely I'd visited any "special place" this close to home, I gasped as we rounded a corner and one of the state's icons came into view atop a rugged, rocky ledge. Starkly white against a darkening cloudbank was a venerable lighthouse that must have guided captains and their vessels to safety for centuries.

"I recognize it from photos and drawings," I said. "But believe it or not, I've never visited this lighthouse."

"It was in pretty bad shape and closed to the public along with the property for as long as I can remember," Connor explained as he pulled into a small paved parking lot. "Looks like we've got some rain comin' through, but we'll see what we can."

The lighthouse itself and walkway up to it was indeed not open to the public. But as Connor and I stood on the edge of the steep cliff it occupied, we watched wave after wave crash below us and appreciated why the beacon had been sited there.

"Imagine you are in a ship off this coast in a pea soup fog," Connor said. "The harbor is here somewhere, but you can't see a damn thing, and you can hear waves smashing on the rocks. It'd be absolutely terrifying. Suddenly, through the murk you see the light that's gonna save your life."

I put my hand on his shoulder. "That's a pretty profound image."

"Want to hear a lighthouse adage?"

"Sure, go ahead."

"Dark in the absence of light is like a problem in the absence of an idea—not absence of a solution."

I stepped back and considered Connor's words. "You think I'm missing something important about Luke."

He nodded. "A question, actually, that our lighthouse here can help us answer."

I shook my head. "I'm totally in the dark."

Grinning, he said, "Yup, that's it."

I threw up my hands. "*What's* it?"

"You suspect that Luke used fish oil to lure a shark to where Cary was swimming. The problem is that oil dissipates pretty fast, so a shark would have to be within a couple of hundred yards or so to detect it. Farther out, they'd be in the dark, you might say."

"But," I added, "Luke could've put chunks of oily bait like bluefish or mackerel in cages under the water. Like the lighthouse, that would draw a shark nearer to shore, and fish oil would bring them in closer still. That's clever, Connor."

He shrugged. "Cops catch bad guys by trying to figure out how they think. The big problem is proving you are right."

I pondered that for a moment and then shook my head. "I can't think how."

"We need inside information from somebody who has spent time in Luke's house—a cook, cleaning lady, someone like that," he said.

Grinning, I said, "I'll bet Malissie knows that."

He nodded, "Brilliant minds, Mara. Brilliant minds. I'll call her when we get home."

I checked out Harvey's roses in the backyard while Connor went inside to look up Malissie's number and use the phone to call her. Fifteen minutes later he stepped onto the deck sporting a Cheshire cat grin.

"Successful?" I asked.

"You betcha. Her name is Daisy."

"Daisy," I repeated.

"Luke's cleaning lady who lives near Malissie. From what you've told me about Luke, I'd guess he'd be a high-and-mighty type boss."

"So Daisy might be willing to share privileged information," I said.

And that's why Connor and I found ourselves sipping tea once more in Malissie's living room, this time with a very talkative Daisy McCarthy. More than willing, Daisy was eager to tell us what she thought of "that bastard" Luke.

After the requisite small talk about possible relatives, Connor asked, "So, Daisy, how long did you work for Luke O'Sullivan?"

Twirling a red braid, she answered, "Three months, and that was three months too long."

"Did he go after you, or what?" I asked.

"He did, but I gave 'im the what for, and he backed off. Worse, it felt like he was watchin' me all the time, like I was gonna steal somethin'."

"That's awful, I said. "You were right to leave. I have a question that might seem kind of odd. Did Luke spend time looking out on the water though binoculars or maybe a telescope?"

"Sure he did," Daisy said. "Once I asked if I could look through the telescope, you know, to see over the ocean. He about lost it. Told me to stay away from that telescope or else."

I shook my head. "How rude. Um, where did Luke use the telescope?"

"On a balcony-like that's off his upstairs study. That way, he said he got a real good view of the whole ocean."

9

To avoid the "damn tourists," Connor took yet another road down to Spruce Harbor. Fifteen minutes into the drive I still hadn't recognized a single landmark, building, or town.

"You know," I said, "I've lived in Maine all my life and thought I knew the state pretty well. But like yesterday, I don't have a clue where we are."

"Ayuh. We got miles and miles of back roads. Take a wrong turn and boom, you don't know where you are."

"And speaking of that, where are we with Luke O'Sullivan and what's next?"

Connor paused for a moment and turned left at a four-way intersection with no obvious landmarks. "With what Daisy said, he's not the nicest guy. But that doesn't make him a killer, of course."

"Right, but where do we go from here?"

"Someone, probably you, needs to get into the water for a look-see," he said.

"Yeah, I was coming to that conclusion myself. The problem is how do I check out Luke's underwater shark snacks without him seeing me."

He smirked. "Sometimes even expert sea kayakers tip over."

"I was afraid you'd come up with that idea," I said.

And so, once again, I drove to Phippsburg along with the kayak and all my gear. Always vigilant about capsizing the boat in Maine water no matter the time of year, I asked Connor to accompany me.

"Seeing who we're dealing with," he'd said, "no way was I gonna let you go alone."

I climbed into the kayak at the put-in and paddled slowly in the direction of Luke's house while Connor walked the dirt path above me. We chatted about nothing much in case anyone overhead us, which was improbable, but you never know.

Directly in front of Luke's mansion I rolled the kayak, thrashed around a bit underwater, pushed myself out of the cockpit, and came up yelping.

Next, Connor and I acted out the scene we'd scripted. He shouted, "Do you need help?"

I yelled back, "I'm okay, but something fell out of my kayak and sank. I need to go down and get it."

Then I unzipped my life jacket, threw it on the deck, swam out a few strokes, and dove down. Only the surface was warm, and I was quickly immersed in icy, gin-clear seawater. Since the bottom was only twenty-odd feet below, I easily saw what was down there, popped back up to the surface, and yelled, "Got it!"

I had to get back in the boat, and given the cold water I blessed the paddle float I always carry on the kayak's stern. Attached to the end of a paddle, the float acts as an outrigger and helps stabilize the tippy boat as a kayaker attempts reentry. It's important to emphasize the word "attempt."

It had been a while since I'd practiced the maneuver, but I gave it a go. First, I slipped the float onto one end of the paddle and positioned the other end behind the seat and perpendicular to the kayak. Hoping I remembered the tricky part, I next floated on my stomach, feet back, and lay both feet onto the floating paddle. After that, I slowly put the closest leg into the kayak cockpit and followed with the other one. Continuing to lean on the outrigger, I managed to corkscrew myself into the seat, turning in the direction of the float.

Grinning to beat the band, I settled into the cockpit, raised the paddle, and laughed at Connor's thumbs up.

Back inside the truck, I toweled off and changed into dry clothes as Connor visited the outhouse. We didn't talk about anything important until the kayak was tied down to the top of the truck and we were on the road.

"Okay," he said, "I'm dying to know what you saw down there."

"The water was really clear and not that deep, so the visibility was good," I said. "It's pretty much what we thought—a dozen or so lobster traps weighted down with something heavy just sitting on the bottom. Fill some traps with bloody meat and put fish or whatever in the others, and you'd have a pretty good shark lure."

"So we're thinking Luke baits his traps, sinks them, and then uses the spotting scope on his balcony to see how quickly the sharks come in. Is that it?"

"Assuming the lure works, it's a pretty simple scheme that wouldn't implicate Luke unless someone gets in the water and pokes around. He'd say he was home looking out at the ocean through his scopes like he always does."

Connor shook his head. "Cripes. I'm really beginning to dislike this guy, and I've never even met 'im."

"We've made excellent progress with good guesses," I said, "but I'm not sure where that gets us. Sinking lobster traps baited with meat is odd, but it's not a crime."

"You got that right," Connor said. "We need to get Luke to recreate what he did to Cary and catch him doing it."

Frowning, I looked at him. "Recreate?"

"You know, do the same thing."

"I know the definition, Connor. It's your meaning I don't get."

He glanced over and shrugged. "I'm workin' out the details in my mind, but the bottom line is that Luke's got to think somebody is on to him."

"I'm guessing," I said, "the somebody will be a female scientist who knew Cary and is poking around to find out what happened."

We were about to unload the kayak in my driveway when Connor snapped his fingers. "Cripes, I almost forgot. Harvey wants you to come over for dinner, and you don't need to bring anything."

"Let's put the boat on the grass next to the garage," I said. "And yes, I'd love to have dinner with you both and not just because my fridge is just about empty."

10

SEATED ON HARVEY'S LIVING ROOM COUCH BEFORE DINNER, I gave her a blow-by-blow description of our discovery and ts implications. Within earshot in the kitchen, Connor readied the steaks he was going to cook on the grill but didn't interrupt.

Harvey frowned. "The part I don't get is the next step. You want Luke to think that you suspect him? Good lord, Mara, the man's paranoid and dangerous. Who knows what someone like that will do?"

Wiping his hands on a dishtowel, Connor stepped into the kitchen doorframe. "Harvey, it's just an idea at this point."

"Right," she said. "Your 'ideas'"—she air quoted the word—"have a way of manifesting themselves. How about the time you took Mara out to that island in your boat where some nut forced her to jump into freezing cold water so she'd drown?"

I shrugged and said, "But I didn't."

Frowning, she asked, "You didn't what?"

"Drown."

Over dessert—wild Maine blueberry pie—Harvey was the first to mention sharks, not me or Connor. "Mara, you should tell Brady MacFarlane about this Luke character and what you've discovered. MacFarlane has studied shark behavior for decades, so he might have an idea how to trick Luke so you don't have to get into the water."

I held up my fork and said, "Harve, that's an excellent idea. And, by the way, this is really good pie."

Visiting scientists at MOI are given special treatment. That includes offices with the best views, and Brady MacFarlane's suite on the top floor of the biology building, which I visited the next morning, was no exception.

Brady's door was partly open, but I knocked anyway. To his "come on in" I stepped into a large space with windows that nearly wrapped around the whole room. Seated behind his desk, Brady grinned and rose as I approached.

"Mara Tusconi," he said. "Hey, I meant to thank you for inviting me to your party. I had a great time and talked to a couple of new folks. But you didn't climb those thirty-seven steps just to chit-chat with me, so what can I do for you?"

"You're right," I said, "and what I'd like to talk with you about is going to take a little time."

He raised an eyebrow. "Now you've got me curious. Help yourself to a chair, and take all the time you need."

And so I laid out the whole story—who Luke O'Sullivan was, that his neighbor Cary loved swimming off the rocks near both their homes, plus Luke's loss of his mother and sister. I ended with a description of the wire traps that, when baited, could lure sharks along with fish oil.

Seated at his desk, Brady took it all in, nodded, and asked a few questions. When I was finished he said, "Mara, I'm so grateful you told me all this. The description of the shark attack on poor Cary made no sense to me. Sharks don't appear out of nowhere to kill people. They just don't, and one of my life missions is to change that misconception. Delusional or not, in my view this Luke character should be shot."

"You won't get a chance to shoot him," I said, "but if you and I work together we might set a trap he'll walk right into."

Brady raised an eyebrow. "Trap, eh? Now, you've *really* got my attention."

Sipping rich coffee brewed by Brady's fancy Keurig coffee machine, we sketched out a plan that capitalized on O'Sullivan's inflated ego. The idea rested on Brady chatting with Luke as the two looked out over the water. Learning that he was talking to a famous shark scientist, we hoped Luke would brag about his genius ability to lure sharks close to shore, something Brady would agree was very hard to do. Asked how in heaven's name he did that, O'Sullivan' would describe the sunken traps, the bait he used, and the final bit of genius—fish oil. The cell phone in Brady's breast pocket would record the whole conversation in case we needed that evidence.

"I think it's a good plan," Brady said. "But how do I get this Luke to stand on the ledge and talk to me?"

"Easy," I said. "Set up an expensive-looking spotting scope on the rocks near his house and the man will be out in a flash."

The next morning on our way to Phippsburg, Brady and I decided it would be a good idea if I stayed behind and waited in the parking lot. Sitting there anxiously, I drummed my fingers on the steering wheel and wondered what was happening. A half hour after he'd left, Brady flipped open the Subaru's hatch, stored his spotting scope, slammed the hatch shut, and slid into the passenger seat.

"Well?" I asked.

Brady shook his head. "No way that guy could've set up that shark lure. He knows squat about sharks, and he's kind of wacky to boot. I didn't talk to him long, of course, but he was all over the place. I'm no psychiatrist, but he came across as a borderline schizophrenic."

"Whoa," I said. "That throws a different light on things. But *someone* set up and baited those traps. If Luke didn't do it, who did and why?"

Brady shrugged. "Truly, I wish I knew. Maybe you need to go back to the lady you called Miss Marple reincarnated. Sounds like she knows everybody and their history. In fact, why don't we stop and see if she's home?"

11

MALISSIE WAS "IN THE BACKYARD TENDING HER garden" according to the butler (or who I thought was her butler, if they still exist). As we circled the house, Brady raised an eyebrow at the size of the Victorian mansion and was even more impressed by the backyard view.

Acting as though we were expected guests, Malissie welcomed us to her humble garden, which was anything but. Roses of every imaginable color—hot pink, rose, raspberry, canary yellow, sky blue, royal blue, apricot—climbed fences, trellises, lattices, and a wall.

Saying, "I was just thinking about taking a little break," Malissie gestured toward several weathered wooden deck chairs that offered a cliff-side view of the water. After Brady introduced himself, I noted that the rose garden was spectacular, which launched Malissie into a ten-minute discourse on the dos and don'ts of growing roses in Maine. After she explained why "a location with eastern exposure is best to protect the leaves from hot afternoon sun," Malissie stopped and added, "but I don't think you came here to talk about roses, did you?"

"I love learning about your flowers," I said, "but we need your help again with who might've set up that shark lure. Brady met Luke, talked with him about sharks, and doesn't think Luke has the, um, intellect to do it."

Looking at Brady, Malissie said, "Hmm. I see what you mean, and you're probably right. That would've taken a good bit of planning."

"So," I said. "If Luke didn't, who did?"

Staring out to sea, Malissie leaned forward in her chair, looked thoughtful for a half-minute, and sat back. "When we were first talking about the O'Sullivan family, I said they were ambitious, which is why they did so well. As I'm sure you know, there's good ambitious and the ruthless kind. To get ahead, the O'Sullivans sometimes stepped over the line—especially Luke's father, Sean."

"I take it he's still around?"

Looking over at me, Malissie nodded. "He's got a home down in Florida and the big house you've seen up this way. So yes, Sean O'Sullivan is here in Phippsburg quite a bit during the summer."

Looking pensive, Brady said, "I'd like to know more about Sean, including how he made his money."

"To be honest," she said, "I'd describe Sean as secretive, pushy, and at times dishonest. And he got rich buying locals' houses, fixing them up a little, renting them, and finally selling them for double the price a year later."

Explaining further, I added, "Brady, a while back folks who made their living on the water, like lobstermen, sold their houses for what seemed like an amazing amount of cash and moved inland. In the short run they did make money, but they lost access to the water, and that turned out to be a big problem."

"Ayuh," Malissie said. "It's a predicament all right that people like Sean O'Sullivan just laugh at."

Pensive, Brady murmured, "Interesting."

I looked over at him. "I don't get how Sean selling houses in less than scrupulous ways helps us with Carrie's murder."

Brady watched a few waves crash against the rocks below us before answering. "I really don't know. It's just intuition at this point."

On the way back to Spruce Harbor, Brady launched into a discourse about the unconscious and scientific discovery. "John Dewey, the education crusader," he said, "wrote some really interesting essays about the role of intuition and imagination in science. One thing he emphasized that's always stuck with me explains how we come up with ideas and solutions. Dewey believed it just kind of happens and isn't as intentional as we might think."

"What some scientists call intuition," I said.

"Right. And most of us leave it there because we don't know where to go with it." With a laugh he added, "I could go on, but I don't want to bore you. Read Dewey's *How We Think* for more information."

It was my turn to laugh. "Brady, you are the last thing from boring."

"Well that's good to hear. A few women I've known said the opposite."

Uncertain how to respond, I didn't. But since "I've known" referred to the past, for the first time I wondered if Brady MacFarlane was presently involved in a romantic relationship.

12

I'D JUST FINISHED PUTTING THE DINNER PLATES IN THE dishwasher when Ted called from Woods Hole. "Hey," I said. "How's it going down there?"

Ted launched into the latest details about the autonomous high-speed gliders he and his Woods Hole colleagues were working on to study ocean warming. Body length and rocket-shaped, the gliders move through the water on preprogrammed routes and measure pretty much anything an oceanographer would want—temperature, salinity, pressure, chlorophyll, current velocity, oxygen. When the glider surfaces, data are transmitted to researchers on a ship via satellites.

The autonomous technology is truly spectacular, but ten minutes into the phone call I'd heard enough. My silence finally gave Ted the message.

"Well, um," he said. "Enough of that. How are things there?"

Given Ted's insistence that I not investigate what happened to Cary, I was vague about my comings and goings over the last few days. "Oh, the usual," I said. "Let's see, Harvey and Connor invited me over for dinner, which was nice. And I met someone who knows all about roses. She's an elderly lady who said she'll help me design a rose garden later this summer."

Ted had no interest in gardens, especially flower ones, so it was no surprise that he asked no follow-up questions about the "elderly lady."

"All right then," he said.

I was about to say, "Miss you, Ted," but the line was dead.

After dinner I enjoyed a mug of herbal tea on the deck and watched stars appear in the darkening sky—the Milky Way, Big Dipper, Orion's Belt, and a planet, maybe Mars—and wondered why I hadn't told Ted the truth about what I'd been doing and just dealt with his response. Did my evasion mean something important about our relationship or not? I mulled that over for a while and concluded that I just didn't know.

The next morning I was in my office when Cary's mother called. It was a good thing I was seated at my desk.

The woman sounded drained. "Mara, I'm afraid I have bad news for you. Caroline died just after eleven last night."

After a gasp I said, "Oh, Mrs. McBride, I am so terribly sorry to hear this and for your loss."

She cleared her throat and added, "I do appreciate that. We are working on details about the service, but it will be held in the Phippsburg Unitarian Church at noon the day after tomorrow. I hope to see you then."

I was about to thank her and add that I would certainly be there, but she'd already ended the call. After hanging up, I stared at the phone. Days ago, Cary McBride was a bright, eager young woman who wanted to be an oceanographer and nothing else. And now she was gone forever. I understood that her death wasn't an accident and the responsible person had to be held accountable. But I didn't know the hard part—how to make that happen.

Once more I climbed the thirty-seven steps up to Brady MacFarlane's office. As usual, Brady was seated behind his desk staring at a computer. He looked up, read my expression, pointed to an adjacent chair, and waited.

"Cary McBride died late last night," I murmured.

He rubbed his forehead for a moment, nodded, and asked, "Tell me what you are thinking."

"I'm thinking Cary was a lovely, bright young scientist with everything ahead of her and that someone cut her life short. And I'm thinking the someone should be punished."

"I agree, of course, that the responsible person deserves punishment," he said. "Of course, the tricky part is figuring out, positively, who that person is."

"Right," I agreed. "And we are smart, creative scientists who work on unknowns all the time. *We* can figure this out."

True to his character, Brady didn't disagree with counter-arguments about lack of evidence and the rest. He simply said, "Okay, so let's give it a go."

We began then and there with chalk and the old blackboard on the wall. At the top of four columns Brady wrote in capital letters "WHO," "WHY," "WHEN," and "NEED TO KNOW." Ten minutes later we'd written "Luke," "Sean," and "Unknown" in the first column and "Paranoia about car accident and female driver," "Real estate ambition," and "Unknown" in the second.

"Let's talk about timing," I said.

Brady nodded. "Go ahead."

I stared at the board. "The sunken traps could be baited anytime, but fish oil dissipates in, what, fifteen or twenty minutes?"

"Correct," Brady agreed.

"Um, that's a problem. Don't you think?"

Brady shrugged. "Not necessarily. There's always polyvinyl alcohol."

"Polyvinyl what?"

"Alcohol."

I rolled my eyes. "Okay. But what is that?"

"A colorless polymer that dissolves in water. The polymer encapsulates laundry powders, spices, flour, you name it, that you use every day. Drop your powder or whatever in water and the polymer slowly liquefies."

"Hold on," I said. "Are you thinking that someone familiar with this polymer could have use used them on fish oil?"

He shrugged. "Why not?"

"But who knows about stuff like that?"

"Anyone familiar with building or renting homes, for one thing," he said.

Across from Sean's name in the "Need To Know" column I wrote, "Did Sean use polyvinyl alcohol containers in his rentals?"

Brady tapped what I'd just written. "Is there anyone who can help us with this?"

"Probably," I said. "Her name is Daisy."

13

FROM BRADY'S OFFICE, I TELEPHONED MALISSIE, GOT Daisy's phone number, called, and left a message asking her to get back to me when she got a chance. Less than five minutes later, Daisy returned my call. I held the cell phone away from my ear so Brady could hear what she was saying.

"That was quick, Daisy, so thanks. I need to ask a question," I said. "Kind of a strange one."

"No problem, Mara. When you work for Sean O'Sullivan, you get used to strange questions."

"Okay," I said. "I understand that Sean rented out some of the houses he owned. Did he hire you to clean them?"

To her "Yes he did," Brady gave me a thumbs up.

"Daisy, here's what I'm wondering. Did Sean stock the bathrooms with things like hand soap, moisturizing cream, and shampoo in those clear containers people use one time?"

"Sure," she answered. "And it was a total pain 'cause people always walked off with those things, and I had ta get more."

"How about single-use laundry soap?"

"Yup," she said. "That too."

"Daisy, that's terrific. You've been a big help."

As if she answered questions about laundry packs and household products every day, Daisy said, "Not a problem. But since I'm not working for Mr. O'Sullivan anymore I won't be able to help, you know, in the future."

"Oh," I said. "Are you moving away?"

"Me move from here? Lordy, no. But I heard Mr. O'Sullivan talkin' on the phone about building more cottages right there since it's such a pretty spot. No way I'll be cleanin' all those rentals."

I thanked Daisy and ended the call as Brady added the new information to our table. Watching him, I said, "Actually, I don't get how knowing Sean had single-use products in his rentals helps us."

Brady shrugged. "It's just an idea, and maybe a not a good one. But something else she said interested me."

To my raised eyebrow he said, "Sean O'Sullivan wants to build more houses so he can rent them out."

"Sorry, Brady. I'm not with you at all."

"An ambitious builder who recognizes the potential of the Phippsburg ledges would do whatever he could to get rid of sharks, don't you think? Especially after what happened to Cary."

"Sure," I said, "but if that's the case why would Sean bait those underwater traps?"

Brady shook his head. "People bait sharks to get close enough to kill them, so maybe *that's* Sean O'Sullivan's game."

"How would he kill a shark?"

"People shoot them, usually with a .22-caliber gun. It's illegal, of course."

I shrugged. "But since owning a gun like that isn't, we still seem to be stuck."

"I've got an idea that will sound pretty crazy, so just bear with me," he said. "If Sean thought he'd succeeded in attracting a shark with his lure, we could catch him in the act of shooting it."

I tried to imagine the scene. "And evidence like photos of Sean shooting a shark could be used against him."

Nodding, Brady said, "Exactly."

"Um, there's a big problem with your scheme, don't you think?"

"Mara, Sean wouldn't be shooting a *real* shark. It'd be a decoy."

I looked around the room. "And you've hidden a decoy shark somewhere?"

"I'll contact the shark experts in Massachusetts," he said. "If anyone knows about something like that, they will."

This time it was my turn to listen in on a call as Brady spoke with his Cape Cod colleagues. "Let me get his straight," the male voice said. "You are asking about a decoy of an actual shark, not one that attracts sharks."

"That's right," Brady said. "A decoy that really looks like a shark."

"We've got a terrific decoy made with a fiberglass skin over a foam-rubber core, but it's a seal. Damn good model, too."

"Uh huh," Brady said. "So can you direct me to someone who has an actual shark decoy?"

"I'd try the folks at the New England Aquarium in Boston. They've got some terrific exhibits."

Four phone calls later, we finally reached the animal display company recommended by the aquarium's education department. Describing the prop, a Miss Miller said, "Our shark model is life-size and *very* realistic."

"We might want to put the prop into seawater," Brady said. "Would that be a problem?"

"Not a bit, Dr. MacFarlane. Our displays are made of durable fiberglass resin designed to withstand all weather conditions. Otherwise they wouldn't be suitable for both outdoor and indoor exhibits, would they?"

After Brady agreed with Miss Miller that she was right, of course, he asked about the prop's price.

"A thousand dollars plus another hundred at least for shipping. Would you like to place an order now?"

Punting with "I need to check with a colleague," Brady promised he'd get back to Miller very soon and ended the call.

"One thousand dollars for a shark model is a lot of dough," I exclaimed. "Do you have that kind of money?"

He nodded. "Oddly enough, I do. My budget includes an education line that I need to spend and could certainly use for a shark model. The grant proposal folks at Scripps will help with the logistics."

"That's great," I said. "But the thing will be huge. Where in heaven's name will you put it?"

"My lab at Scripps is pretty large—plenty of space to hang Miss Miller."

To my raised eyebrow, he added, "That's what I'll call the model, of course."

14

CARY'S MEMORIAL SERVICE WAS HELD LATER THAT AFTER-noon in the Phippsburg Unitarian Church. When Harvey and I arrived, the church was nearly full, but we found seats in a side pew near the back and waited for the ceremony to begin. In the spirit of inclusive Unitarianism, during the service there was very little mention of a deity. Instead, Cary's family and close friends spoke of dignity, peace, and each person's inherent worth.

I managed not to cry until Cary's father, Christopher McBride, described his daughter's passion for the ocean. Gripping the podium, he said, "Cary loved nothing more than being in the water. She wasn't even ten when she told us she was going to be an oceanographer." Blinking, he added, "Big word and big dreams for a little girl. And she'd just stepped into that dream when she…" Shaking his head, the devastated man walked away from the podium as the rest of us wept with him.

The reception was in the church basement, and Harvey and I left soon after speaking briefly with Cary's parents. As we drove out of town, Harvey said she'd like to see "where it took place." After I parked the car, we walked along the ledge, and I described the scene.

"It all happened so fast," I said. "Ted and I were paddling along, and I'd just pointed out that big house behind us. I remember Ted saying it looked more like it belonged in Hollywood than Maine. Then we saw someone swimming alongside the ledge, and as we paddled closer I guessed it was Cary. Suddenly, the swimmer disappeared below the surface and came up screaming. It was just horrible, and you could see blood in the water. Somehow we managed to drape Cary over my bow—she wasn't conscious by then. Ted called for an ambulance, and the medics came very quickly. In the parking lot, they put Cary onto a stretcher, and that was the last time I saw her."

We stopped walking and looked out over the water. "Mara, that's absolutely ghastly—much more real here, of course. And now you think you and Brady might have figured who was responsible and how they did it?"

It took me ten minutes to describe sunken traps that could be baited with meat, how fish oil worked as a shark attractant, who Sean and Luke were, and about Malissie and Daisy.

"That's quite a tortuous account, so let's see if I've got this right," Harvey said. "Based on what you learned from Daisy and Malissie, you believe this Sean is the, um, person of interest."

"That's correct," I said. "And Brady's convinced a developer like Sean would want to attract sharks so he could get rid of them."

"Get rid of them," Harvey repeated.

"Sharks in the water aren't exactly a draw for prospective buyers, right?"

She shrugged. "Of course."

"So we're going use a shark model to test that hypothesis."

"A shark model," she repeated.

"A life-size one that really looks like a shark under the water," I explained.

Staring down into the water, she frowned. "But you said this Sean person lives right near here, so how in heaven's name are you going to get a full-scale shark model in the water and sink it?"

"Right," I said. "That tricky bit is something I hope Connor can help me with."

As I parked in front of her house in Spruce Harbor, Harvey suggested I come in for lemonade and blueberry pound cake. "Connor's truck is here, so he is too. Knowing Connor, he'll come up with a workable plan for the shark ruse before your plate is clean."

She was right, but only because I'd taken a second slice of cake.

"We can use my boat," Connor said. "She's forty feet, so there's plenty of space for your shark decoy on the platform behind the cabin. And we can load it at the MOI dock."

I nodded. "Sounds good. The model is Brady MacFarlane's, so he'll come with us. I'm sure he'll figure out how to submerge the thing before we go, and he'll handle those logistics once we are there."

Sitting back in his kitchen chair, Connor grinned. "Mara, this is just grand. I've been feeling a tad bored, and this little adventure'll give us a whale of a time."

"Shark, not whale," I said, "and that's a very good thing."

I pulled into the MOI parking lot and was happy to see Brady's top floor office brightly lit. Deploying the shark model was a major logistical problem, and he'd be very relieved to hear about the solution.

Nodding, Brady listened to my overview. When I'd finished, he clapped his hands and grinned. "Excellent, Mara, just excellent. Connor sounds like just the right man for the job. Irish, too, which makes it even better."

I ignored the Irish connection. "Besides having the right kind of boat and knowing the waters around here, Connor was a cop before he retired. He's dealt with a lot of shady guys and is more than happy to help Sean O'Sullivan get what he deserves."

15

NOW THAT WE HAD A BASIC PLAN IN PLACE, BRADY AND I needed to work on what he called "the particulars."

"Particular number one is delivery of the shark model," I said. "When will it get here?"

He grinned. "Way ahead of you. Delivery is tomorrow morning between nine and ten. I wonder if we can get Miss Miller onto Connor's boat late in the day, around seven maybe? That way we can deploy her just after dark."

"I'll call Connor when we finish here," I said. "But I bet that'll work for him. Let's see, that model will be pretty buoyant, so what's the plan for weighing it down?"

"Weights attached to the four fins," he said. "I've got a pretty good idea how much weight we'll need so Miss Miller floats a little below the water line with her dorsal fin visible above the surface."

"And how do we keep her from floating away?"

"She'll be anchored to the bottom. I'll get in the water with her at the deployment site to make sure she's anchored properly."

"Anything else?" I asked.

He looked out one of his windows. "Is there a shed or small garage behind this building where I can get Miss Miller ready?"

"There is," I said. "I'll talk to Harvey's secretary and figure out the logistics of using it."

Turning, Brady looked at me and grinned. "Mara Tusconi, it's terrific working on all this with you. I haven't had this much fun in a long time."

Leaving Brady's office, I realized that the declaration applied to me as well.

The following day, I was amazed how every aspect of the "Miss Miller Operation" fell right into place. The animal display company arrived on time, and two guys carried the fifteen-foot model into an empty carpenter's garage, waited for Brady's signature, thanked him for their tip, and drove off. Within view of the MOI dock, the garage was a good place for Brady to prepare the decoy. From there, we could easily carry it onto Connor's boat.

The only snag had been negotiating my call with Ted the night before. He'd often remarked that "trouble followed me around," which, though partly true, I found extremely irritating. For that reason, I couldn't very well tell him the whole shark-Sean-decoy-Connor's boat story. What I did tell him was a partial truth—that I was looking forward to a "really nice sunset boat ride with Connor."

Two hours before sunset, I watched Connor motor up to MOI's dock and tie his bow and stern lines around the pilings. Together we walked into the garage so Connor could meet Brady and take a look at the decoy.

Connor and Brady talked about the logistics of floating the decoy just below the surface. Lifting the decoy to get an idea of its weight, Connor grinned and said, "Well, Miss Miller, I've never had a shark aboard my boat and hope to God I'll not have another. Jus' behave yourself and we'll get along fine."

We pulled away from the dock as the sun began to slip below the horizon. That way we'd have just enough light to motor over to Phippsburg, find a good deployment location, and anchor. After dark we could take our time lowering the weighted decoy into the water. Snorkeling around, Brady planned to use a waterproof dive light to make sure Miss Miller was securely attached to the bottom and floating below the surface with her dorsal fin exposed.

It all went according to plan until Brady was about to get back into the boat from the stern so we could head home. Connor and I couldn't see a thing with his blinding spotlight, but the bellowed order from Sean O'Sullivan was absolutely clear.

"Stop what the hell you're doin'! Hands up!"

I nearly fainted. But Connor, who'd dealt with plenty of bullies, called out, "We've a lobster boat here with a bit of engine trouble, mate, so we drifted all the ways over heah. Give us a second, and we'll be gone, eh?"

Hearing the Irish brogue, Sean turned sympathetic. "Engine trouble, ya say?"

The exchange gave Brady enough time to slip under the boat and climb up the side facing away from Sean. With Brady safely aboard, Connor started the engine, slowly backed away from shore, waved at Sean, steered toward Spruce Harbor, and took off.

In the wheelhouse, I said, "Connor, that was awesome!" After toweling off and getting dressed, Brady winked at me. Then he put his hand on Connor's shoulder and said, "Thank you, sir. That went even better than I expected."

To both compliments, Connor just shrugged, but his grin gave him away.

16

CONNOR TIED OFF HIS BOAT AT MOI's DOCK AND suggested we head over to the Lea Side for a "wee celebration." After Brady and I agreed, Connor called Harvey, who reportedly was "dying to hear what happened" and would meet us at the restaurant.

The Lea Side was busy, but we found an empty booth in the back. Famished, I placed a double order of the night's fish and chips special, which Brady promised he'd help me eat. As Connor and Brady enjoyed their Maine ale and I my wine, Harvey plied us with questions.

"So," she said, "this decoy shark is now anchored to the bottom and floating just below the surface?"

"That's right, "Brady said. "With her dorsal fin sticking out of the water. We call our decoy Miss Miller, by the way."

Nonplussed by Brady's explanation of the nickname, Harvey said, "I see. Now, what happens next?"

"Well," he said, "in the perfect scenario, this Sean O'Sullivan will see our shark tomorrow morning, freak out, and try to shoot it."

"That's illegal, I take it?"

"Sharks are protected by the 2011 Shark Conservation Act," Brady said. "That law specifically bans shark finning."

"I'm not sure what that is," Harvey said. "It sounds pretty bad."

"People cut off a shark's fin and throw the rest of the animal back into the water to die. Every year, something like seventy million sharks end up in people's soup bowls that way."

Eyes wide, Harvey whispered, "Good lord."

"The point is that great white sharks have federal protection," Brady said. "If someone like O'Sullivan takes aim and shoots one, I'll go after the bastard."

I reached for a French fry. "Hey, guys, I'm still eating, so maybe we should talk about something besides dead sharks?"

Gracious as always, Harvey asked, "So, Brady, are you enjoying Maine? It's a big change from California."

"I like it a lot," he said. "There're more people in San Diego than in the whole state of Maine. Here you've got wide-open spaces, quiet beaches, unpolluted water, and clean air. Plus the people are, I don't know, more real."

Teasing, I said, "Gosh, it sounds like you'd like to move here."

His wistful response took me by surprise. "More than you know, Mara, more than you know."

After we'd finished our meals, the waitress asked if we'd like dessert and cleared the table when we all declined. Brady stated that he was "absolutely bushed" and left not long after that. Saying he'd be right back, Connor headed for the bathroom, which left Harvey and me alone until he returned.

"So," she said. "Brady would like to live here."

I shrugged. "Maine is vacationland. Says so on our license plates."

"Mara," she said, "for a smart woman you can be pretty dense."

"And you can be frustratingly obtuse," I said. "Dense about what?"

"Okay, I'll just say it. Brady MacFarlane is in love with you."

I sat back in the booth and crossed my arms. "Get off it, Harvey. We are just colleagues and friends, nothing more."

"Connor's on his way back," she said. "We can talk about this tomorrow."

That night Harvey's proclamation haunted me, and I simply couldn't fall asleep. Was she right, and had I completely misread Brady's "just the person I want to see"-type statements? And what about me? Did I have "feelings" for Brady I hadn't acknowledged? Had I unconsciously led him on?

The next morning, I expected my scheduled phone call with Ted to help, but that was not to be. When I asked which day he'd be home, Ted cleared his throat and said, "Actually, Mara, there's been a major change in the ship schedule. We're leaving two weeks early. Something about faulty drill bits for the hydraulic piston corers, which means the geochemists had to rearrange their coring schedule. Since those folks are paying for the ship time, there's nothing I can do about it."

"Whoa," I said. "So you won't be back for a while then?"

"Afraid not," he said. "It'll be a good while now. Sorry, gotta go."

Confused about what had just happened, I put down the phone. It was unusual for Ted to be curt, and his attitude was unsettling and inexplicable.

Unless we were swamped with work at MOI, Harvey and I made a point of checking in with each other every day. Upended by Ted's new cruise schedule and confused about the "Brady situation," I really wanted—no, needed—to talk with her.

I first tried Harvey's office, where I was greeted by a locked door. My next stop, the biology department, was also unfruitful because the secretary had been "tied up" (whatever that meant) all morning and hadn't seen Harvey. I finally found Harvey in the lab's instrument analysis room. Seeing me, she mouthed "two minutes," so I took a seat at the lab workbench to wait. *Marine Chemists' Analytical Methods,* the book Cary had dubbed "a bible," lay open across from me. Slowly closing it, I whispered, "You would've been a terrific oceanographer."

When Harvey exited "the cell," she walked over to the table and put her hand on the analytical methods book. "I'll return it to the shelf sometime, but not just yet. Um, are you up for some fresh air?"

So, once more, we headed for our patch of green with the water view.

I played with a couple of blades of grass. "Ted called this morning. I was hoping he'd be home next week, but there's a change in the ship's schedule. Something to do with hydraulic piston corers and broken drill bits. Sounds like he won't be back anytime soon."

"I'm sorry to hear that, Mara."

"Yeah. And, um, what you said about Brady. That really upset me. I've tried to figure out if I, you know, led him on. I don't think so. I really don't."

She reached over and put her hand on my arm. "We've agreed to be open and honest with each other, which means that sometimes we'll get it wrong. I really didn't mean to offend you."

I squeezed her hand. "Of course you didn't, and I very much appreciate your saying that."

17

BACK IN MY OFFICE AFTER LUNCH I WAS STARING AT nothing out the window when a knock interrupted my musings.

Brady opened the door just enough to stick his head in. "Mara, do you have a minute?"

I tamped down my usual degree of friendliness. "Oh, hi. What's up?"

He didn't appear to notice my change in tone and walked in. "Next week my shark colleagues in Massachusetts will be tagging sharks off Cape Cod, and they've asked me to join them."

"That's great. You've done it before, I assume?"

He nodded. "Sure, but off California. The thing is there's room for another scientist, and I was wondering if you'd like to go."

Normally, I would've said something like, "Are you kidding?" But, "Um, well, I'm not sure," was all I could manage.

"I know it's short notice," he said. "But these guys are the best of the best. It's an amazing process." He looked at me expectantly.

"The thing is Ted called this morning with news about an uncertain cruise schedule, so he's not sure when he'll be back from Woods Hole. I'd really like to be here when he is so, you know, I can't plan anything for the next week."

With a shrug, Brady said, "Right. Guess we'll just have to wait." With a "see ya later," he turned and was gone.

I stared at the open door and wondered how things had gotten this complicated so quickly. Just two days ago Brady and I had come up with the Miss Miller idea, and we'd deployed the decoy only yesterday. And now—I paused. "Now what?" I whispered. As far as Brady was concerned, nothing had changed. Now it was up to me to figure out if anything had, and for that I needed to clear my head with a hike.

More a hill than a mountain, Spruce Mountain's steep drop-off at the summit offers a pretty view of Spruce Harbor. At the trailhead, I parked along the road and started up a dirt path that steepened a quarter-mile later. Freeing my mind of sharks, men, and other distractions, I paid special attention to loose rocks and what was in bloom (white daisies, purple thistles, yellow buttercups). Fifteen minutes later I scrambled onto the granite outcrop at the top of the trail.

To my left, the Maine Oceanographic Institute dominated the view. Dedicated to ocean research, exploration, and education, MOI was established in the 1950s after the Second World War. My parents were proud to be among the first scientists who worked there, and an inscription at the biology building's entrance credits their vision and dedication. That Bridget and Carlos Tusconi's passion for marine research lived inside me was a privilege I never forgot.

Since sharks were on my mind, I wondered if my parents had ever met Eugene Clark, an ichthyologist who used scuba diving for research and especially for studies of shark behavior. Had Bridget and Carlos ever joined the "Shark Lady" on an oceanographic shark expedition off Florida or maybe the Bahamas? If Clark had invited them, surely they would have gone.

And with that realization I knew there was no question I would join the shark research cruise.

The message on my office phone erased any lingering guilt I may have had about that decision. Saying he'd get back to me when he could, Ted announced that he would board the WHOI research vessel the following day for a month-long cruise.

Brady was halfway down the stairs from his office when I met him on my way up.

"Good news, Brady. I can join you and the shark folks after all. Ted's ship leaves tomorrow, and he'll be gone for at least a month."

Grinning, he gave me a thumbs up. "Terrific, Mara. Just terrific. I haven't worked out the logistics with them yet, and you can help me with that."

Up in his office Brady had tacked a good-sized nautical map of New England waters onto a pegboard. He put the eraser end of a pencil on Cape Cod's eastern coast. "Last year the scientists you'll meet tagged roughly a hundred great white sharks off the National Seashore here, and their data show that about twenty percent of those tagged sharks migrated up to the Gulf of Maine."

With the tip of my forefinger I traced that route. "Okay, imagine there's a shark just south of Provincetown on Cape Cod. To get to Phippsburg, it would swim pretty much due north across the Gulf of Maine past Portland and on up."

He nodded. "Yes. And looking at this chart, you can see why Phippsburg probably isn't the safest place to swim."

I touched a spit of land near where Cary had been bitten. "Cary lived here and swam off the rocks in front of her house. Good lord, a shark swimming up to Maine from the south would arrive at Cary's swimming spot before anywhere else on the Phippsburg peninsula."

Brady shook his head. "That poor girl couldn't have picked a more dangerous place to get into the water."

18

W HILE BRADY USED HIS KEURIG TO MAKE COFFEE I stared at the nautical chart and tried to imagine a great white shark swimming north from Cape Cod. As we sipped our brew I asked Brady to explain how great whites swim.

"It's similar to how airplanes fly," he began. "Like a plane, a shark needs to keep moving forward or it will sink. The back and forth sweep of that powerful tail propels a shark forward, and it uses the front fins to maintain vertical position in the water."

"So sharks tilt the fins down to dive and up to rise," I said.

He nodded. "Exactly. And the dorsal fin on their back acts as a rudder, again akin to a plane."

"I'm trying to picture the shark making its way from Cape Cod up to Maine," I said. "It swims fast, I get that, but why swim all that way?"

Brady walked over to the Keurig, refilled his mug, and came back. "Seals are one of the great white's favorite foods and harbor seals are very abundant along Maine's rocky coast and islands. That alone would be a very good reason for them to visit Maine."

"One more question and then we can figure out the logistics," I said.

Sipping the coffee, he walked over to the chart and traced the shark's likely route. "No reason to apologize, Mara. I love talking about sharks."

I nodded. "Okay. The sharks are swimming north, heading for Maine. How do they know where to go?"

"That," he said, "used to be the million-dollar question. We know now that great whites have an amazing sense of smell. The olfactory lobes in their brains are so large some scientists have dubbed them 'brains of smell.' Great white sharks can detect—smell—prey a quarter-mile away given the right conditions. That's more sensitive than our best chemical analysis."

"Impressive," I said. "Um, a while back I read something about a suite of shark attacks off New Jersey. I think it was in the early nineteen hundreds. Do you know why it happened?"

He nodded. "It was called the terrifying shark attacks of 1916. Hotel guests were swimming (they called it bathing then) off the beaches of Atlantic City up to New Jersey. They wore dark bathing costumes, mostly black and gray, which attracted sharks on the lookout for seals. Worse, the hotels dumped food waste into the water, and that brought in the sharks as well. Four people died and one was injured."

"So Sean's sunken traps full of dead fish would've brought a shark right to Cary's swimming spot," I said.

Brady nodded, "An olfactory version of McDonald's golden arches."

I shook my head. "Enough sharks for now. Let's figure out how to meet up with your colleagues."

As we looked at the chart it was pretty obvious where we should rendezvous with the shark researchers. "From Cape Cod," I said, "their boat will go right by Portland as they head up the coast. The Portland Marine Lab has a dock, and I'm sure they'll let us leave a car in the parking lot for the day."

"Sounds like a plan," Brady said. "I've scheduled a call this evening to arrange the logistics, including timing. How long is the drive from here down to Portland?"

I shrugged. "Well, that depends on the traffic. Midweek though, it shouldn't be more than four hours. One last question," I added. "What kind of vessel are we talking about? Even this time of year Maine waters are pretty chilly. Do I need to bring heavy duty foul weather gear, or can I get away with something lighter?"

He shrugged. "It's a decent sized boat with a large cabin and lots of deck space, so you shouldn't need winter gear. Mostly we'll be deploying acoustic receivers that capture data from sharks already tagged. You won't get wet doing that. But we'll tag a few sharks if we can, and that's an amazing process."

I was home making dinner when my computer's ping announced an incoming email. Hoping it was from Ted, I sat down with a glass of wine at the kitchen table, scanned my messages, and read the most recent one.

"Hi, Mara," it read. "I'm checking in. All good here. The weather is excellent, which helps a lot as you know. We've been steaming to our first station off the Carolinas and can begin work later this evening. It looked like we'd be short one scientist, but a grad student changed her plans and was able to come. Seems real sharp, Ted."

I responded with, "It's terrific; all is going well. Get back to me when you can," and left it at that.

19

OUR RENDEZVOUS WITH THE SHARK RESEARCH TEAM WAS perfectly timed. Brady and I had waited less than fifteen minutes at the Marine Lab dock when their boat rounded a stone pier and headed our way. As Brady promised, it was a good-sized vessel of fifty-plus feet with plenty of fore and aft deck space and a large cabin.

After a crewmate had wrapped the boat's bow and stern lines around the dock's pilings, an athletic-looking woman with raven-black hair pulled up into a ponytail and a ready smile stepped onto the dock to greet us.

She said, "Brady, lovely to see you," and turned to me. "Dr. Tusconi, I'm Roxanne Keeting, and do call me by my first name. So happy to meet you, and thanks for taking the time."

"No better way to spend an afternoon than on the water," I said. "And it's Mara, please."

She nodded. "Let's stash your gear in the cabin, and we can chat there."

As Brady promised, the cabin was spacious and comfortable. Its motors gurgling, the vessel slowly pulled away from the dock and headed north.

Seated on comfy padded benches, I asked Roxanne about her shark research colleagues. She explained that the team included scientists from three institutions in Woods Hole—the NOAA Fisheries Laboratory, Marine Biological Laboratory (MBL), and Woods Hole Oceanographic Institution (WHOI).

"Woods Hole sounds like a pretty special place," I said. "Hundreds of scientists in a charming little Cape Cod town on Vineyard Sound. My partner, Ted, is at WHOI for the year."

She tipped her head. "Huh, I thought you and Brady…." She cleared her throat and said, "Woods Hole *is* special. For the most part, everyone is generous with their time and resources. A couple of weeks ago I needed help with an outdated water sampler I was partial to that wasn't working. The thing must've been twenty-five years old, but it was a good friend, if you know what I mean. It only took a couple of phone calls for me to find this elderly gentleman who worked in the basement of one the MBL buildings. He called my sampler a 'venerable old mate' and fixed it in twenty minutes."

I nodded. "Yeah, I'm still using plankton nets decades old because they've been good to me. So let's talk about what you folks are up to, starting with tagging, which I know very little about."

"Sure," Roxanne said. "We've been tagging great whites in shallow water off Chatham on the southern tip of Cape Cod. The sharks are swimming freely, so we're not catching them. We chum the water with some dead fish to draw a shark close to the boat, reach over the side, and insert a dart into the thick muscle on the shark's back."

"Whoa," I said. "I can't imagine what being so close to a great white is like."

"They are beautiful, graceful animals we need to know more about, Mara. The acoustic tags give us a lot of pretty basic infor-mation—where these sharks spend most of their time, where and when they come and go, that type of thing. For example, we've learned that great whites are migrants that move north and south off the Atlantic coast."

"How about timing?" I asked.

She grinned. "In New England these sharks are like snow bunnies. During cold months, we find them in waters off Florida, and they swim back north around late May. By December they head back down to Florida."

"Of the sharks you've tagged, how many end up off Maine?" I asked.

"About twenty percent. We've got a rough idea where they go in Maine waters, and now we need to sharpen that picture. You know, habitats they might prefer, how close to shore they typically are, and other any patterns we can detect."

"And what's your plan for today?"

"We're not tagging. Brady thought we were, so I hope you aren't disappointed. We are very curious to see where the young lady was when the shark attacked her to get an idea of the water depth, type of habitat, that kind of thing."

"Sure," I said. "I can show you the exact location, and her name is Cary."

Roxanne nodded. "Cary. Let's climb up to the viewing platform as we head out of the harbor. There are some binoculars there and a detailed chart."

Positioned on top of the cabin, the platform offered a panoramic view of Portland Harbor and everything beyond. After we motored away from the city and passed Peaks, Great Diamond, Long, and Chebeague Islands, I pointed to a small, rocky island topped with an expansive green lawn and an enormous house.

"That's the retirement home of polar explorer Admiral Robert Peary, where he retired in the early 1900s. He traveled all the way to the North Pole, and I'm not sure why he ended up there," I said. "We'll go another five miles or so before we get to Phippsburg."

20

W E MOTORED PAST TWO LONG FINGERS OF LAND jutting out into Casco Bay. "Those are the Harpswell and Bailey Island peninsulas," I said, "so we are very near where Cary was bitten." I pointed north. "The big beach way up there with the buildings behind is Popham State Park Beach, and it'd be a good idea if we went a little slower now."

After Roxanne relayed the message, the captain reduced our speed. I spread the chart out on makeshift table, scanned the shoreline with the binocs, and tried to connect what I was seeing with the chart in front of me.

I handed the binoculars to Brady. "Directly in front of us there's a parking lot. I'd say Cary was bitten no more than a half-mile to the left, back towards Portland."

Still looking through the field glasses, he nodded. "Yup, that's it. I can see the huge house up behind there."

Roxanne leaned over the railing and asked the captain to slowly head toward shore in the direction of the O'Sullivan mansion. We came within a few hundred feet from shore when the ship slid to a stop, its engines bubbling.

It took me a minute, but using the binoculars I spotted a fin sticking out of the water to the south a few hundred feet. I handed the binocs to Brady and pointed. "I'm pretty sure I see Miss Miller right there. Maybe two hundred feet beyond the O'Sullivan house."

While Brady scanned the water looking for the fin, I told a very curious Roxanne about Miss Miller, including her name and the ruse we had set to catch Sean O'Sullivan.

"Fascinating," she said. "A shark decoy in the water, dorsal fin exposed, to bring down this Sean character. And, um, we're about as close to shore and we can get, so why don't you describe the ecology right there."

I closed my eyes and imagined being underwater. "Let's see, the water is very clear, and where it's shallow the bottom was sandy with a scatter of smallish rocks. There is a lot of bladderwrack, *Fucus vesiculosus,* and rockweed, *Ascophyllum.* The kelps, *Laminaria* and *Alaria*, are only in deeper water, and their blades are very long, especially *Alaria,* which is ten feet, maybe more. I didn't swim out very far, but you can see from here that there are very large boulders, lots of waves, and heavy surf in the deeper water."

Roxanne nodded. "In a nutshell, the water is clear and cold. Seaweeds like rockweed and kelps are abundant in shallow water, and farther out you find kelps. There's heavy surf and less seaweed where the water is deeper."

"Exactly right," I said. "I'm no shark expert, but this doesn't look like shark habitat to me."

She looked back toward shore and nodded. "In New Zealand sharks sometimes go after seals in kelp forests, but in water a lot deeper than this."

"But you see sharks in shallow water off the Cape, right?"

"Worldwide, it's not that unusual to see sharks where there are surfers and swimmers. In Massachusetts we see them off beaches on the outer Cape, often attacking seals. As you can imagine, that draws a crowd, and it's a good lesson for people who might be cavalier about being out there. And speaking of seeing sharks up close, Mara, are you a scuba diver?"

"Sure," I said. "I used to dive here quite a bit, but lately the cold water has put me off diving. Getting old, I guess."

She grinned. "The dry suit is a total pain, and it's stunning how cold your head can get. But how about diving in warm water?"

I shrugged. "That sounds lovely, but I've never done it."

"We can change that. Florida has some of the best shark diving in the world, which is why Eugenie Clark wanted to establish the Mote Marine Lab there. As I'm sure you know, she was a brilliant, creative scientist. I mean, who would even think to train sharks to push a button for food and show the world how intelligent they are?"

"No question," I said. "Clark was a remarkable person."

She leaned toward me. "Mara, I dive off Florida pretty often to observe sharks. You should fly down and join me."

Not sure what to say, I punted. "It does get pretty cold up here in the winter. Florida would be nice change."

"It's not an offer I frequently make, and I'm serious," she said.

I nodded. "Thank you, Roxanne. I'm sorry if I sounded cavalier. Seeing sharks in their natural habitat would be the dive of a lifetime for me, winter or summer. I'll think seriously about your offer and get back to you."

Brady pointed toward shore. "Roxanne, anything else you'd like to take a look at here?"

She shook her head. "Let's head back to Portland and talk about what we've seen."

Once more we filed into the cabin with the cushy seats. Rubbing her arms, Roxanne said, "Didn't realize how chilly it was up there."

Brady got right down to it. "Okay, Roxanne. What's your take on where Cary was attacked by the shark?"

"It's not typical shark habitat, that's for sure. And I wouldn't expect to find seals there either. Bottom line, someone drew that shark close to shore."

"Like bait in those traps I saw and fish oil poured onto the surface of the water," I said.

"We don't know what's happening with Sean," I added. "But I can probably find out and will let you know if I do."

21

ACK AT MAINE MARINE'S DOCK, BRADY AND I WATCHED the boat until it rounded the stone jetty and was out of sight. Checking his wristwatch, Brady said, "It's nearly six. How about we get dinner somewhere in Portland?"

I pushed aside an image of Brady and I seated in a restaurant's dark corner drinking wine by candlelight. "You know, I'd rather head back to Spruce Harbor and eat at the Lea Side. Is that okay?"

"For sure," he said. "Lea Side it is."

Once more, we slid into one of the Lea Side's booths, listened to the waitress, and chose the night's special—seafood stew—which she promised had "lots of shrimp, clams, and mussels." We also ordered drinks, white wine for me and a Maine beer for Brady.

After lifting the glass to my nose, I took a sip and savored the wine. "Very nice Gavi."

Brady raised his eyebrows. "Isn't that kind of a fancy wine for a place like this?"

I shrugged. "The bartender knows I like it, and now he keeps it on hand for me."

Brady swirled his mug of beer. "No bar I know in California would do that. Your bartender is just the type of person that makes Spruce Harbor so special and why I'd like to live here."

"But you've got a permanent position at Scripps, right? How could you walk away from that?"

He looked to the side as if someone might overhear us. "Don't tell a soul about this, but I've talked to Dixon about my working here. He's looking into it, but seemed very interested."

"Really?"

Grinning, he rolled his eyes. "You needn't sound so surprised."

I backpedaled. "I mean…that is. Um, Dixon is usually pretty circumspect about a new position."

"Mara, I'm teasing you. Of course Dixon will go through proper channels for any hire. The thing is, nobody here at MOI works on large fish like sharks, and I've got an excellent track record for getting grants. At the very least, I think he would offer me something temporary and take it from there."

"Brady, you are a wonderful colleague, and MOI would be very lucky to have you as a scientist, visiting or otherwise." To steer the conversation in a very different direction I asked, "Um, what did you think of Roxanne's offer?"

He winked. "Hey, if you go down to Florida to dive with Roxanne, I'm coming along."

I dropped Brady off at his apartment, another MOI perk for visiting scientists, headed home, and pondered Brady's news that he would not be returning to California anytime soon. It was one of those yin yang things. Brady was a great guy and terrific colleague, so how could I be anything but happy that he'd be at MOI a good deal longer than I expected?

"Admit it," I whispered. "It would be a lot easier if he left because…." But I just couldn't say it aloud.

The next morning, I woke to the sound of my phone ringing. Groggy, I pushed myself to a seated position, grabbed it, and had barely managed a "hullo" when Connor started talking.

"Top o' the morning," Mara. "Got good news."

"Hi, Connor. What's up?"

"Excellent news about Sean O'Sullivan. I tried calling soon after I heard, but you weren't home. Yesterday morning Maine Marine Patrol caught the dumb head trying to shoot that decoy with a rifle. Nine in the mornin' if you can believe that."

"Wow, that *is* excellent. So what's going to happen to Sean now?"

"Don't know, but I'll find out what I can," he said. "At the least, Sean will get a whopping fine, but the publicity won't do him any good."

"Publicity?"

"The news guys are gonna be all over this, and I'd think shooting a rifle into the water in broad daylight wouldn't be good publicity for house sales right there."

"Huh," I said. "See what you mean."

"Doesn't this mean your Miss Miller has done her bit, and you need help gettin' her back to MOI?"

"Yes, sure," I said.

"I'm up for another boat ride, so why don't you talk to your shark buddy about when he'd like to rescue his dummy and get back to me?"

An hour later I climbed the stairs to Brady's office, found the door wide open, knocked on it, and stuck my head in. Seated at his desk, Brady was frowning at a computer screen and didn't hear my knock. So I tried a different tack.

"Ground control to Major Tom."

That got his attention, and he looked up smiling. "One of David Bowie's best songs."

Pulling the chair against the wall closer to Brady's desk, I said, "I have no idea what it means."

"Want the short or long version"?

I sat down. "Let's go with the short one for now."

"Um, let's see. Major Tom, not a real person, blasts into space, loses contact with ground control, and gets lost. Some people interpret this as Bowie getting high and, you know, losing control."

I nearly said, "Like I've lost control," but I caught myself in time.

22

BRADY GRINNED. "I'M SURE YOU DIDN'T CLIMB THOSE stairs to learn about Major Tom. What's up?"

"Connor called this morning with interesting news. Apparently, Marine Patrol caught Sean trying to shoot the decoy in broad daylight. I have no idea what regulations he ignored, but I hope they throw the book at him."

"At the very least, he discharged a firearm within a few hundred feet of a dwelling," Brady said. "That's pretty serious."

I shrugged. "Connor can find out. And speaking of Connor, he's offered to take us back to Phippsburg so we can retrieve Miss Miller. The timing is up to us."

"Anytime tomorrow works for me," he said. "I've got a half dozen research papers I promised to critique and return to colleagues today. You know how that is. The boat trip will motivate me to get it done."

I stood. "Excellent. I'll call Connor. Is the same time as before good with you?"

"Perfect." He winked. "I'll look forward to spending tomorrow with you, Connor, and Miss Miller."

I unlocked the door to my office only to be greeted by three research papers I had promised to critique and return to the lead authors the day before. Mumbling, "Shoot them a quick note saying they'll be a day late," I brought my computer to life, opened my email, and sent three messages into cyberspace.

I barely had time to be pleased with myself when the phone rang. It was Ted.

"Hey," I said. "Good to hear from you. Are you still at sea?"

In the background a woman's voice called out his name, but I couldn't hear his response because he muffled the phone.

"Sorry about that," he said. "We're heading back to Woods Hole now."

"Which means you'll be back home soon?"

He didn't answer, so I asked, "Ted, you still there?"

Clearing his throat, he said, "Yeah. Actually, I'm not sure when I'll go back up there."

"So there's lots of work to do after you dock."

"Yeah, there is, but that's not the reason."

I frowned at the phone. "Ted, I'm not following you."

"It's just, Um, I mean…Damn it, Mara, I've met someone. That's the reason."

I couldn't speak.

"Mara, you still there?"

I cleared my throat and said, "Yes, Ted. I'm still here."

"You've got to understand that I didn't want this to happen."

The anger bubbled up. "That's crap. It happened because you let it."

Suddenly, all I could hear was static, and then the line was dead. I stared at the phone for a moment, slammed the receiver onto the cradle, and left my office. Fifteen minutes later, I parked my car at the base of Spruce Mountain, sprinted up the trail, and leaned against the granite outcrop, chest heaving.

Finally, I pulled myself together and tried to analyze the crisis I hadn't seen coming. Were there any signs Ted was unhappy that I'd missed? Had I done anything to anger him? And how about me—unaware, had I distanced myself from Ted?

The last question stopped me cold. I had to admit that recently Brady MacFarlane was on my mind a good deal more than Ted. And while I hadn't done anything to be ashamed of, my feelings for Brady were very real and growing.

"Maybe," I whispered aloud, "that's happened for a reason you didn't want to admit to."

Back down at sea level, I drove toward MOI when Harvey passed me heading the other way. I turned around, followed her home, and pulled up behind her truck as she was climbing out of it.

Startled, she said, "Mara! What are you doing here?"

I opened my door and walked over to her. "Please, Harve. I need, no *have*, to talk to you."

Baffled, she frowned and then said, "Oh, Lord. Has someone died? Angelo?"

I shook my head. "No, no, Angelo is fine. It's Ted. He says he's in love with someone else."

Instantly in charge, she put an arm around my shoulder. "Let's go into the house and have some hot tea. Connor is off somewhere, so we have the place to ourselves."

Seated at Harvey's kitchen table, I sipped hot, sweet tea and told her what I knew and how I felt. When we had finished, she asked a few questions.

"Ted was definite in what he said about the, um, student?"

Nodding, I added, "And that he didn't know when he'd be back here."

"And you realize now that you might have feelings for Brady MacFarlane, but you haven't acted on them?"

The insinuation irritated me. "No, Harvey, the only thing Brady and I have shared is dinner after the shark trip."

"Look, Mara. I'm not accusing you of anything. I'm just trying to understand what's going on here."

I shrugged. "Sorry. I'm feeling pretty bad, as you can imagine."

"Actually, Mara, I can't imagine how you feel. This is all so sudden. How about talking to Angelo? He knows you better than anyone and loves you like a daughter, of course."

Perhaps it was the word "love" that brought tears to my eyes. Dabbing them with a tissue, I nodded. "Yes, I want to talk with Angelo. He's always been my rock, and boy do I need solid and stable right now."

At the tip of Seal Point, Angelo's house commanded an outstanding view of Spruce Harbor and beyond. He was a retired marine engineer who'd loved talking to my parents about things like ocean currents, deep sea trenches, and the latest in marine technology. As a child, I often escaped such boring adult talk, pressed my nose against Angelo's window panes, watched ships until they disappeared from view, and imagined where they went.

I ran up his stone steps, pulled open the oak door, and stepped into his impressively large kitchen. I'd called him before leaving Harvey's house, so he was expecting me. Per usual in midsummer, he stood at the sink scaling fish.

He looked over his shoulder in my direction. "Mara, it's lovely to see you of course, but I don't think you'd welcome a hug from me at the moment. Take a seat, and I'll be right with you."

23

SEATED AT HIS OLD PINE TABLE, I WATCHED MY GODFATHER work. A handsome Italian, with curly white hair and blue-gray eyes, Angelo de Luca was one of those people who never seemed to age. Whether he was ducking a sailboat's boom on a jibe or cutting out fish bones with his fillet knife, Angelo's actions were quick and precise.

Finished with the fish, he washed his hands, toweled them dry, sat down across from me, and reached over to squeeze my hands for a moment.

"Something's gone very wrong, Mara. You sounded pretty upset on the phone."

Between sobs it all came out—Ted's phone call and sudden announcement plus my disbelief, anger, and uncertainty about the future.

"I'm so very sorry, Mara, I really am. You may not be ready to hear this right now, but you'll get through this. I know you will. Ah, you mentioned someone named Brady when you called. He's the shark scientist Connor told me all about, the one who set out that shark decoy?"

Nodding, I dabbed my nose and said, "That's right. Brady MacFarlane."

Now, I don't want to put you on the spot, Mara, but from how you talked about him earlier and what Connor said, I take it he's more than just a colleague."

"But we haven't...um...."

Angelo interrupted me. "Please. I know that. *Cio che deve succedere.*"

"Sorry, my Italian's a little rusty."

"What will be, will be. In other words, Mara, perhaps this is some kind of fate. Ted may have closed one door, but there is another one open for you."

As Angelo prepared and cooked the Italian version of fried fish—olive oil with garlic, onion, tomatoes, black olives, fresh parsley, and wine—I wondered if he was right. If so, it certainly wouldn't have been the first time.

After drinking a little more wine than usual, I slept surprisingly well that night. In the morning I carried my mug of steaming coffee out to the deck, leaned on the railing, took in the view, and considered my situation. Notwithstanding recent events, I was unquestionably a very lucky woman. I lived in a great place, worked with terrific colleagues in a venerable marine laboratory, and enjoyed excellent health. Sure, Ted's behavior was dreadful, but I was strong and could—no, would—move on.

Seated at my office desk, I'd just shut down my computer when Brady knocked on the door and leaned in.

"'Morning, Mara. Is this a good time?"

"Brady, hi. I just sent off the last of my tardy reviews, so yes."

He stepped in. "I was hoping Connor talked to you about retrieving the shark model."

"Actually, yes. I had dinner with Harvey and Connor last night. He'll be happy to motor us back there pretty much anytime."

With a thumbs up, Brady said, "Great. The weather looks good today and the tide is right."

And so, once more, Connor picked Brady and me up at the MOI dock and motored us over to Phippsburg. Given her size, it was a struggle to get Miss Miller up and over the transom of Connor's boat, but with Brady pushing her aft end from the water and Connor pulling from above, the model finally fell onto the deck.

That done, Connor turned to me. "Are Sean's traps still down there?"

I shrugged. "Far as I know."

Connor leaned over the side to speak with Brady. "Those lobster traps are probably still on the bottom, and nobody is taking care of them. It'd be awful if a lobster crawled in and couldn't escape from a trap."

Brady treaded water and nodded. "I'll get the traps, no problem."

Fifteen minutes later, Connor stacked the empty traps against the transom while Brady climbed into the boat. In the cabin, Connor started up the motor for our trip home while Brady toweled off.

Trying not to stare at his body, I said, "Why don't I give you some privacy so you can get into on some dry clothes?"

He grinned. "If you don't mind, that would be, um, easier."

While Brady was getting dressed, I walked to the stern and looked back toward Phippsburg. Was it only a couple of weeks since I first paddled there with Maureen and Sarah? In those few days my life had turned upside down.

I whispered to myself, "What Ted did totally sucks and it hurts. But you made it through a disaster a whole lot worse than this one and can do it again."

At the MOI dock, Connor and Brady wrestled the unwieldy model onto the dock and carried it into the garage where it had been stored.

As Connor sped off, Brady stood in the MOI parking lot and rubbed his damp hair.

"After I go home and take a shower, how about we have dinner at the Lea Side?"

With nothing to stop me, I didn't hesitate. "For sure. Meet you there in an hour?"

24

I WALKED INTO THE LEA SIDE, SAID HI TO JOEY, AND WAITED while he poured me a glass of what he called "Mara's wine." Handing me the glass, Joey pointed to a booth with a view of the water and said, "He's there."

Sliding into the booth, I said, "Good choice, water view. Just curious, did you ask Joey to direct me back here?"

Brady grinned. "No, and that he did confirms what I said earlier about living here. People know who you are, even outsiders like me."

I rolled my eyes. "Just because you have a temporary position, that doesn't mean you are an outsider."

Swirling his mug of beer, he tipped his head to the side. "Speaking of temporary, I spoke with Dixon again today."

I leaned toward him. "And?"

As if his announcement were a secret, Brady whispered, "It's a go. He has extended my appointment for a year."

I grasped his free hand. "That's fantastic news. Just fantastic."

Once more we ordered the dinner special, Italian seafood stew. We both declined dessert, but I ordered a glass of champagne while Brady stayed with beer.

After I toasted his good news, Brady leaned closer. "Something's happened."

That took me by surprise. Harvey was the only person who read me so easily.

I took another sip of champagne. "Um, good call. I spoke with Ted yesterday. He's in love with someone else."

Brady sucked in a breath and whispered, "Oh my god." Speaking louder he added, "And you? How are you doing?"

I shrugged. "I've been talking to the people closest to me—Harvey, Connor, and my godfather Angelo—and that's helped a lot. The thing is, I never saw this coming and wonder if I should have."

Brady shook his head. "Ted is a god-damned fool. Please don't tell me she's a grad student."

"Bingo," I said.

Taking my hand again, Brady cleaned closer. "Mara, you are a remarkable, beautiful, smart woman, *and* a terrific scientist. Any man would be incredibly lucky to have you as his partner."

I blinked back tears. "Brady, thank you so very much for saying that. It means the world to me."

After work the next day, I channeled my anger toward Ted into something productive—expunging all traces of him from my house. I carried three cardboard boxes filled with clothes, shoes, bathroom supplies, books, plus his special wine bottle opener, into the garage, piled them on top of one another in a corner, walked back into the kitchen, and closed my eyes for a moment. Once more, this was *my* house and that felt absolutely okay.

To celebrate, the next morning I climbed the stairs to Brady's office and asked if he'd like to come over for dinner with me that evening.

Seated at his desk, he looked up from his computer and grinned. "I can't imagine a better invitation, Mara. Did you want to go out again?"

"Actually, I was thinking we'd have a picnic on an island not far off my beach. We can paddle out there in my kayaks."

"That'd be a real treat. What can I bring?"

"Not a thing, except wear a bathing suit if you want to go

for a swim, and bring dry clothes because it can get pretty chilly out there. I'll stuff some beach towels in one of the boat hatches. Um, we better be on the water by five so we have plenty of light for the paddle back."

It'd been a very long time since I'd planned a picnic dinner, and I splurged on lobster rolls plus watermelon salad, lemon coconut bars, chips, beer for Brady, wine for me, and seltzer water. By the time Brady arrived, I'd packed the food and other dinner things, plus towels, a beach blanket, and my clothes, into both kayaks' hatches. We added his gear and carried the kayaks down to the beach one at a time along with our paddles.

On the water, I pointed to an island a half-mile off shore. "That's our destination. We can kayak around later if you want, but let's get set up and eat first."

As we approached the island Brady said, "How about a quick swim before we eat?"

I nodded. "That sounds good. The tide is going down, so we don't need to carry the boats up too far."

One by one, we carried the kayaks up the beach past the seaweed line. Already wearing our bathing suits, we sprinted to the water and dove in. I was floating on my back when Brady came up with a yelp.

"Yikes! This water's a lot colder than where I was swimming with Miss Miller."

"Well," I said, "we're off the Maine coast now. Water temps are in the mid-fifties off Portland now and probably colder than that here."

He swam over and pulled me close. "Mmm, Mara. Nice and warm."

And, for the first time, we kissed.

25

OPENING MY EYES, I PULLED BACK A BIT AND SAID, "UM, there's a beach towel in your aft hatch."

Brady was already toweling off when I climbed out of the water. He opened the hatch on his kayak, pulled out a small duffel bag, and pointed to a sizeable rock behind us. "I'll go behind that erratic there, change, and give you some privacy. Let me know when you are all set."

Grateful for his thoughtfulness, I retrieved my own bag, pulled off my bathing suit, toweled quickly, and changed into dry clothes. Rubbing my hair with the towel, I called out, "I'm decent!"

He walked over to the kayak. "Let's get this dinner set up, shall we? I'm pretty hungry."

While Brady spread the blanket over a level area of sand, I placed a towel next to my kayak and arranged the food. Pointing to each item, I said, "There's lobster rolls, chips, watermelon salad, seltzer water, and beer and wine. Plus paper plates, forks, napkins, and cups."

"No dessert?" Brady teased.

"Right, I forgot. Lemon coconut bars."

Before eating, we toasted each other with beer and wine. "To our good health," we said in unison.

Lounging on the blanket, we took our time and savored every part of the meal.

I held up my half-eaten lobster roll. "You could say this drives Maine's economy in the summer, at least along the coast. How do you like it?"

"Believe it or not," he said, "this is my very first lobster roll. It's very good, of course, but also very rich. Not the kind of thing you eat every week."

A lobster roll, some salad, and a half-glass of wine later, I declared I was full. "Brady, the coconut bars are all for you."

"Maybe later. Let's get this food back into the kayak."

That done, we lay back down on the blanket. Stroking my hair, Brady said, "Warning, Mara Tusconi. I'm having a hard time keeping away from you."

The sky was beginning to darken when we loaded everything into the boats and carried them into the water. As the kayaks slid up onto the beach in front of my house, a hot red sun sank down below the horizon.

I rubbed my arms and said, "Come up to the house and take a hot shower."

"Now that's an invitation you only need to make once."

While Brady showered upstairs, I washed off quickly in the downstairs shower and changed. Warm and dry, we chatted across the kitchen table over hot tea and the remaining two lemon bars.

It was pushing nine when Brady said, "Well, guess I better go."

I reached over and grasped his hand. "Why don't you stay the night?"

His eyes widened. "Are you sure?"

"Absolutely, definitely, categorically sure."

Brady was still asleep when I woke up the next morning, so I rolled out of bed, grabbed my clothes, tiptoed out of the room, and dressed downstairs. Wearing only his jeans, Brady shuffled into the kitchen where I was setting the table.

Blinking, he said, "Morning. Um, I'd kill for a cup of coffee."

I handed him a mug. "Ground coffee is already in the filter next to the sink, and hot water's in the kettle on the stove. Can you manage pour-through before you've had your caffeine?"

He took the mug and kissed me on the cheek. "Pour-through coffee before my caffeine. That's good. And yes, I can manage."

Brady made his coffee and leaned back against the counter to drink it.

You know," I said, "despite the, um, things we've shared, I have no idea what you eat for breakfast."

He smirked but didn't take the bait. "My breakfast cuisine is quite broad. I eat pretty much anything."

"That's good since I can only offer you eggs and toast together or separately."

"Mara, together is better. Very much better."

Over the next week Brady and I fell into a comfortable, easy routine. We rode into MOI together and, for the most part, holed up in our respective offices to work on research papers, grant proposals, and other projects with looming deadlines. Twice we sat next to each other in the auditorium and listened to visiting speakers. In need of caffeine on a couple of occasions, we walked over to the Lea Side for coffee. At the end of the day we rode back to my house together, stopping at the grocery store as we needed to.

If any of my colleagues noticed anything out of the ordinary, they didn't say.

We'd been at this for several days when I stopped at the bottom of the biology building's steps on our way back from the Lea Side and said, "You haven't met Homer yet. Is this a good time?"

Brady rolled his eyes. "And Homer is…?"

"It's hard to explain," I said, "but we need to go down to the basement."

Mumbling, "the basement," Brady followed me into the building, down the basement steps, through double swinging doors, and into a cavernous, noisy space.

"Let's wait here for a bit," I said. "Close your eyes and take it in."

A good sport, Brady said, "Sure, Mara. It's your show."

A half-minute later I said, "Okay. Any observations?"

He blinked his eyes open. "Um, a hint of caramel and citrus?"

"Very funny, Brady. I'm serious."

"Let's see. It is super loud and smells like brine."

I nodded. "This place always brings back memories of my father. I was five when he first brought me down here. The roar of the water was loud, and he had to shout. We looked into an aquarium with baby lobsters zipping around, and he asked what they looked like. Saying 'superman,' I leaned over and put my arms out front. He laughed, and I asked what little lobsters ate. He tried to describe all the microscopic creatures we couldn't see."

He turned to face me. "When it's right, I'd love to hear more about your parents."

I nodded. "Sure, and it's past time that you met Angelo de Luca, my godfather, but first you must meet Homer, my friend and confidant."

"Homer," Brady repeated.

Walking, I said over my shoulder, "*Homarus americanus*, and he's back here."

26

HOMER'S AQUARIUM WAS THE LARGER THAN ALL THE others, as befits a long-bodied crustacean with overly big front claws. Per usual, he was nestled in the back corner, seemingly asleep, although I couldn't know that for sure.

I put my hand on Brady's arm. "If you tap quietly on the tank, he'll probably walk over."

A scuba diver, Brady knew firsthand how loud sound could be underwater, and his tap was very gentle.

Moments later, Homer tiptoed to the front of the tank on his eight walking legs and waited. When I touched my finger to the glass, he matched the greeting with his antenna.

I whispered, "Brady, there are mussels in an aquarium we passed. Could you crush a couple and drop the flesh into the tank? Homer will love you for it."

Brady gently floated mussel meat onto the surface and watched Homer snatch each piece before it hit the bottom, shred it with his ripper claw, and use one of his walking legs to move the food to his mouthparts.

"You know," Brady said, "I've never actually watched how lobsters eat. This is very cool. So do you come down here often?"

"Usually when something's wrong and I'm upset. This will sound silly, but it always seems like Homer is a good listener, and I leave feeling better."

He took my hand. "Not silly in the least. Many animals relate to humans more than most of us appreciate. For the most part, we don't even realize it."

When I called Angelo that afternoon he answered on the second ring.

"Mara, good. I've been thinking about you, of course. How are you?"

"Much better than the last time you saw me," I said. "Does dinner at your house tonight work for you?"

"Yes it does, my dear."

"Um, I'll bring someone I want you to meet."

"The shark expert?"

Smiling, I said, "Can't get a thing past you, can I?"

"For me, you are a *libro aperto*, my dear. I will see you both around six, and I very much look forward to it."

On our way to Angelo's house, I told Brady a little about my godfather.

"He's a retired marine engineer and very smart. My parents died in that awful submersible accident when I was nineteen, and I was absolutely devastated, of course. Angelo's home became my own; he was so patient and understanding. I can't imagine what I would've done without him."

Brady reached over from the passenger seat and squeezed my shoulder. "It will be an honor to meet him, Mara. It really will."

Angelo is an avid fisherman, and he and Brady quickly identified what I call "all things fish" as a shared passion. As I made salad and otherwise helped with dinner, the two men spoke a foreign language. Truly, surge tubes, large spoons, and sankos mean absolutely nothing to me. But the best timing and location for catching fish was another matter because terms such as peak tide and sediment type were standard marine terminology.

I was staring out the kitchen window sipping my wine when my godfather finally noticed my absence from the conversation.

"Well, Brady," Angelo said, "next time Connor and I go out for stripers, maybe you can join us."

Nodding, Brady said, "I'd love to, sir."

"It's Angelo, please. Now, who's ready for pesce alla puttanesca?"

During the ride home, Brady talked nonstop about Angelo. "What a terrific guy! I felt completely comfortable right away, and I'd love to go fishing with him and Connor. And that was the best fish puttanesca I've ever had."

Realizing I couldn't be more pleased, I reached over and squeezed his hand.

27

THE NEXT MORNING AFTER BREAKFAST, BRADY READ THE local paper and sipped his second cup of coffee while I puttered around the kitchen and cleaned up. I'd just finished when he said, "There's an article here about scuba diving in Maine. A place called Biddeford Pool?"

I pulled up the chair opposite him. "I've snorkeled there. It's a sandy beach with a steady decline to a depth of about thirty-odd feet. Pretty tame diving for you, I'd say."

He shrugged. "That doesn't matter; it would still be fun. We could look for the yellow lobster."

"Yellow lobster?" I repeated.

"Named Banana. Very rare, something like one in thirty million. Some Biddeford lobsterman swears he caught one in a trap and threw it back. More to the point, is your scuba certification up to date?"

"Sure is, and I keep the gear in my lab. There's three tanks, plus regulators, weight belts, wetsuits, dive flag, and all the rest. Check it out today and see what you think."

That afternoon Brady took his time inspecting O-rings, gauges, hoses, and second stage breathing operation of the tanks and regulators, plus buoyancy gear, dive weights, and harnesses.

I watched him move from one piece of equipment to the next and said, "All this gear makes you realize how foreign and dangerous being underwater is for us air-breathing creatures."

Kneeling next to a tank, he looked up at me. "You are absolutely right. Too many people forget that scuba diving *is* very dangerous, and the deeper you go, the more dangerous it gets."

I nodded. "Biddeford Pool is pretty shallow, depending on the tide. It's best to go on a calm day because the waves can become breakers when the wind picks up."

He stood. "Any idea what the weather forecast is for tomorrow?"

"At this point, it sounds perfect. Sunny without much wind."

"Okay, let's load your car up with this gear and whatever else you'll need," he said. "I've got my mask plus a shorty wetsuit and fins in my lab."

Maine weather is notoriously difficult to predict. But this time the weather gurus had it right, and we woke up to a sunny day with low wind. High tide was at noon, and by eleven-thirty we'd carried our gear to the waterline, wiggled into shorty wetsuits, and pulled on our fins. After I secured a weight belt around my waist, Brady helped me with my scuba tank.

"Can you manage your own tank?" I asked.

"Yup," he said. "And I'll take care of the dive flag too. Let me know if you need help with your mask."

Facing away from the water, I rubbed some spit on the inside of the mask's lens, put the mask on top of my head, pulled it down over my face, and secured the strap behind my head. At that point, Brady's tank was already in place and he was tightening the strap.

"You good to go?" he asked.

I gave him the diver's "okay" signal—thumb and forefinger in a circle, the other fingers extending up.

Then, going backwards in the awkward fins, we walked into the waves. When the water was shoulder depth for me, Brady pointed away from shore, swam out a little ways, and treaded water until I'd paddled out to him.

He pulled the snorkel out of his mouth. "Good to go?"

When I answered with the diver's "okay" again, we replaced our snorkels with scuba tank regulators, floated on our bellies, sank down below the waves, and slowly headed out to sea.

The water was less turbid beneath the surface, and its clarity increased the deeper we went. At a depth of what I guessed was ten feet, Brady touched my arm again to make sure I was all right. Nodding, I pointed toward the open ocean but shrugged when I pointed downward.

Brady responded with the "okay" sign once again. He understood that I wasn't sure how deep I wanted to go.

Gliding forward, I looked from side to side. The bottom was mostly sand with a scatter of small boulders and green leafy seaweed. Small brown crabs scurried this way and that as we floated by. When the water deepened, brown rockweeds replaced the green algae. Brady touched my arm and pointed at a normal-colored lobster backing underneath a boulder.

After ten minutes or so, we reached a cliff where the bottom fell away and the water was very clear. Brady touched my arm, and I watched him let out line so the dive flag would remain visible to anyone on the surface. We slowly followed a rock ledge down about twenty additional feet where a school of cunner fish scattered as we approached and more crabs than I could count scurried under the nearest ledge. Little blue fish I couldn't identify fled every which way. Brady touched my arm again and pointed to a striking red anemone, its tentacles swaying, hanging upside down beneath an overhang. Nodding, I pointed up. We'd gone deep enough, and I wanted to head back to shallower water.

Brady gave me the "okay" sign again. An experienced diver, he knew how quickly time passed on a scuba dive.

Doing our route in reverse, I followed the ledge up to where it leveled off and turned toward what I assumed was the beach. Brady floated alongside and pointed in the same direction, indicating that my assumption was correct. Since it was very, very easy to become disoriented underwater, a second opinion could be a lifesaver.

Brady checked the gauges on both our tanks and nodded. We had plenty of air for the return trip and could take our time.

More quickly than I expected, the water became shallower and more turbid as we glided over the boulders and brown crabs. Once we reached the sand, I pulled off my fins, took the regulator out of my mouth, stood in the shallow water, and waited for Brady, who was behind me.

Floating up, he said, "Hey, could you take the dive flag? I can't manage it and get my fins off at the same time."

That done, we splashed through the shallow water, dragging our fins, the flag, and our dive masks as we stumbled to shore. When we reached the beach, I plopped down on the sand.

28

I PUSHED MY HAIR UP OFF MY FOREHEAD. "BRADY, THAT WAS probably the easiest dive you've ever done, but I hope it was fun."

He grinned. "It *was* fun, and on a dive, easy can be good. There're too many things that can go wrong and then, boom, you are in trouble."

"Let's sit here for a bit while I catch my breath," I said. "So on dives you've done, what's gone wrong?"

He shrugged. "It's obviously really bad if your dive buddy's equipment fails for some reason and you are seventy-five feet down. We've all practiced sharing a regulator from a single tank—that's standard scuba training—but it's a whole 'nother thing when it happens for real and you are deep. Besides sharing the regulator and not hogging it, you've got to ascend slowly, as usual, or you'll get the bends."

"I can imagine. You'd just want to get up into open air."

"You got that right. Depth is another thing. When the dive is exciting, like in a blue hole or something, it's real easy to not pay attention to your depth gauge. Suddenly, you are a hundred feet down when you never meant to go that deep."

"How about marine animals?"

He grinned. "I assume you don't mean sharks. When you dive in the tropics, there are lots of critters that can sting, poke, and bite you. I know firsthand how fire coral got its name. Sea urchin spines hurt like the devil too. Then there's dangerous fish like triggerfish, lionfish, clownfish, and the list goes on."

Suddenly feeling itchy, I changed the subject. "Um, as you saw, Biddeford Pool is a popular Maine dive site because it's pretty and not difficult. Experienced divers who want a challenge go way up to Eastport. That's the easternmost city in Maine and in the country, and you can even see Canada from there. It's very rocky, and apparently divers follow a wall down. Someone looking for a challenge could also go up to Acadia National Park. I've heard that the sea life is terrific—bright red anemones, purple starfish, orange corals, pink sponges."

Standing, he said, "Huh. So you don't have to go down to the tropics to see colors like that. I had no idea."

We carried the dive gear up to the parking lot, dried everything off as well as we could, and put everything on the rubber mat in the back of my Subaru wagon.

Brushing sand off his butt, Brady asked, "Would you like me to sit on a towel?"

"That's up to you," I said. "Leather seats clean up pretty easily. And it wouldn't be the first time this car has gotten sandy and wet. It's usually kayak stuff—paddles, booties, life jackets, wetsuits, and all the rest."

On the way home I reminded Brady that he'd offered to cook dinner that evening.

"I didn't forget," he said. "I've been trying to decide what to make. How does *cacciucco* sound?"

"It sounds Italian, but I've no idea what it is."

"*Cacciucco* is a traditional stew from Tuscany with octopus, mussels, shrimp, calamari, and fish, of course—red snapper and monkfish usually, but I substitute cod, hake, or halibut. Tonight, I'll also add some lobster. You cook it all with tomatoes, fish stock, wine, garlic, plus some red chili flakes."

"Yum," I said. "The fish store will have everything but the octopus. And, to tell you the truth, I'll never eat one."

"I'm with you on that. Why in the world would you eat a highly intelligent animal that can distinguish shapes, quickly make its way through mazes, and is a master aquarium escape artist?"

I nodded. "The octopus that escaped from the New Zealand aquarium through a drainpipe into the Pacific Ocean made the headlines."

Seated at the kitchen table that evening, I watched Brady prepare and begin to cook the *cacciucco*. "Smelling really good," I said. "A girl could get used to this."

He turned away from the stove for a moment, winked, said, "That's the plan," and returned to his culinary duties.

"Speaking of plan," I said, "there are a couple of classic summer Maine events you might be interested in."

"If you don't mind speaking to my back while I cook, I'd like to hear about that."

"You'd love the Lobster Festival in Rockland, especially the lobster boat and lobster crate races."

He faced me again. "I know what a lobster boat race is, but lobster crates?"

"I suppose that *is* kind of confusing. The crates don't go anywhere. There's a string of fifty greased, partly submerged lobster crates people try to run across without falling in. It's incredibly hard to do, but one year I watched a young woman run back and forth, back and forth something like twenty times before she fell off."

"That'd be something to watch," Brady said. "And speaking of lobster, dinner is ready."

29

THE NEXT DAY AFTER WORK I ASKED BRADY IF HE'D LIKE to walk up Spruce Mountain.

"It's called a mountain by locals, but it's really only a hill. The view is pretty nice, though."

"Hey," he said, "just because I'm from California doesn't mean I think all mountains are thousands of feet high."

When we reached the top, I showed him the obvious landmarks. "You can see the twin headlands that protect Spruce Harbor and make it such a terrific port, and that big red bell buoy straight ahead is the Juniper Ledge buoy. On our way back to Spruce Harbor from a cruise, I always listen for the clang of that buoy because it tells me we're back home before I can see the harbor itself."

Brady pointed to MOI. "You can see all of it from up here—the ships, docks, outbuildings, and the main lab. On the ground it doesn't seem quite so big."

"It's a pretty impressive place," I agreed. "Looking down at the lab, I always think about my parents. Carlos and Bridget Tusconi were among the founding MOI scientists."

He put his hand on my shoulder. "I hardly know anything about your mother and father, Mara. It must be painful to talk about them."

"That's true," I said, "but Angelo has helped a lot. He tells me what they were like when they were younger, dating, and all that."

He squeezed my shoulder and took a step back. "And what *were* they like? If it's okay to talk about them, I mean."

I shrugged. "It's okay. They were already well into their thirties when they got married, which is why I don't have siblings, I guess. Angelo told me Bridget Shea Tusconi was so beautiful she lit up the room. Carlos would do anything to help someone. They were both smart and loved doing marine research."

Brady shook his head. "And you were only nineteen when they died."

"Yes. I basically retreated from the world and buried myself in work. There was lots to do—grad school exams, my doctoral research at sea, grant proposals and research papers to write, a job to secure. After that, more grant proposals, research papers, time at sea, professional meetings to attend."

"And you ended up with the perfect job at Maine's only oceanographic institution, so it paid off."

Shading my eyes, I looked out over the harbor again. "That's true, of course. But I haven't taken much time to, you know, just live. Harvey has helped with that."

"You've mentioned a couple of times that your parents died in a submarine accident. Do you mind if I ask what happened?"

I turned to face him. "It was similar to the *Johnson Sea Link* accident in the early seventies. A carbon dioxide scrubber failed, and the pilot couldn't surface because the sub was stuck beneath some kind of overhang. Mom and Dad died of asphyxiation."

"Good lord," Brady whispered as he pulled me close.

That evening neither of us had to cook because Harvey had invited us for cocktails and dinner. On the way there, I told Brady a little about her background.

"Harvey's parents are very wealthy. She went to a private high school and expensive New England college. You may have noticed that she wears posh clothes—cashmere sweaters, designer pants, expensive shoes, that kind of thing."

Brady shrugged. "To tell you the truth, I don't notice the type of clothes anyone wears."

I grinned. "So what do you notice about someone?"

"Um, what kind of vehicle they own, for one thing. And Harvey drives an expensive red Toyota Tundra with aluminum wheels and all the rest."

"Plus?" I asked.

He nodded. "A rifle on the gun rack."

"Bingo," I said. "Very observant."

Harvey opened the front door before we had a chance to ring her bell. "Hey, you two. Connor is in the kitchen making dinner, so I've got you all to myself for a little while. Mara, why don't you lead the way into the living room. Um, I know Mara will drink white wine, but what about you, Brady?"

"Do you have Rising Tide's IPA?"

"It's the one with the guy rowing a boat on the label, right?"

He grinned. "That's the one, Harvey."

Brady followed me into the living room where we settled onto a cushy couch.

"Harvey always amazes me," I said. "She doesn't even drink beer, so how does she know the beer you asked for has 'the guy rowing a boat on the label'?"

Brady shrugged. "Connor?"

I shook my head. "Don't think so. If Connor is drinking a Maine beer, it'd be Gritty's."

Harvey handed us our drinks and joined us on the couch. "So what have you two been up to? Besides work, I mean."

"Well, we did a scuba dive down in Biddeford," I said.

"That's awesome and something I've never done," she said. "Brady, I want to hear all about it."

And so, for the next ten minutes, I listened while Brady described the dive in detail and Harvey interrupted with questions about the equipment, depth, colors, and every marine animal we saw along the way. Watching them both, I realized how lucky I was to have such a warm, inquisitive friend and generous, loving partner.

The word *partner* stayed with me until Brady finished his account. This was the first time I'd thought of Brady as my partner, and I liked the sound of it very much indeed.

30

IT WAS PUSHING FIVE THE NEXT DAY WHEN I CLIMBED THE stairs to Brady's office, walked in, and waited as he finished talking to someone on the phone.

After ending the call, he said, "That was an invitation to dinner this evening with a visiting scientist. I'm sure you could come if you'd like."

"Maybe," I said. "What kind of a scientist?"

"He studies the evolution of elasmobranchs. You know, rays, skates, sharks."

I gave him my best eye roll. "While I do know what elasmobranchs are, their study isn't top on my list of fascinating topics. So I'll give it a pass. Can you get a ride home okay?"

"I'm sure someone can do that. See you no later than ten."

My expectation of a quiet evening on my own was shattered when I pulled into the driveway and parked next to a gray truck. Unannounced, Ted was back from Woods Hole.

I walked up onto the deck where he was seated, a glass of beer in his hand. Tapping the glass, he asked, "You are a beer drinker now?"

I ignored the question. "Ted, what the hell are you doing here?"

"Hey," he slurred. "Don't I live here?"

I crossed my arms. "That's a privilege you walked away from, as you know very well."

With a flick of his hand, Ted discarded the comment. "There's men's jeans in the dryer. Brady's, I assume."

"Let me refresh your memory, Ted McKnight. You called me from Woods Hole with news that you'd fallen in love with a grad student. There was no discussion then, and there won't be now. Get the hell out of here, or I'll call the police. And when you leave, take the cardboard box in the garage. That's where I put your books and clothes."

I stomped past him, walked into the kitchen, slammed the door, and locked it. Later when I looked out, Ted's car was gone.

When Brady found me, I was seated outside on the deck staring at the few remaining wisps of crimson left by the setting sun. He knelt beside me and grasped my hand. "What's happened?"

I wet my lips. "Ted was here when I got home. He took his things, and now he's gone."

Brady shook his head. "Mara, that must have been awful."

I blinked back tears. "*He* was awful. Arrogant, like he owned the place."

"I don't know Ted at all," Brady said, "but maybe he realizes he completely blew it and is acting defensive as a kind of cover-up. Um, is there anyone you can talk to who might help?"

Standing, I replied, "Tomorrow, Harvey and Angelo. Right now I just want to go to bed and have you hold me."

In the morning, I phoned Angelo to ask if I could stop by after work.

"*Ovviamente*," he said. "Of course."

Guessing that something was wrong, when I arrived Angelo already had tea and my favorite Italian almond cookies, amaretti, on the kitchen table.

Trying unsuccessfully not to sniffle, I ignored the food and started to tell him what happened.

Predictably, my godfather said, "Hot drink and sweet first, Mara, and then we can talk about Ted."

And, as always, Angelo was right. The tea and almond cookie did help me feel better. I settled back in my chair and waited for what I guessed was coming.

Reaching across the table, he took both my hands. "You won't be surprised when I admit to doubts I had about Ted from the beginning. While there was nothing obvious, he never showed those little affections for you that I'd expect from someone in love. You know, things like hand squeezes, a peck on the cheek, a smile from across the room. Early on, I put it to his Scottish heritage, but as time went by that reason didn't seem right. I came to the conclusion that Ted McKnight was not a warm person willing to give of himself and therefore not the man you deserved."

Still holding Angelo's hands, I leaned closer to him. The hint of blue in his silver-gray eyes had turned them a steel color.

"But you kept that to yourself," I said.

"Thinking back, perhaps that was a mistake, but I assumed that you knew the man better than I did."

I looked to the side. "It appears I really didn't know him well at all."

"No, Mara. You knew what he let you see. He hid something, and you mustn't blame yourself for that." And with that, Angelo released my hands. "Enough sadness. Let's enjoy sweets and tea while you tell me the latest about your Brady."

I left Angelo's kitchen an hour later with a cookie-sweet high and more hopeful perspective on my life. It was time to look forward, appreciate all that I had, and leave behind regrets and a man I apparently never really knew.

31

THE FOLLOWING DAY IT WAS ALREADY PUSHING FIVE P.M. when Brady and I carried our grocery bags into the kitchen and slid them onto the countertop.

"While I get dinner going," he said, "you can put everything else away. Then why don't you sit out on the deck and wonder about some excellent news?"

Seated in one of the deck stairs, I watched the sky turn crimson as the sun slid down into the water and tried to imagine what Brady's news might be. Perhaps one of his grant proposals had been funded or maybe he'd been invited to give a talk someplace exotic.

By the time he settled onto the stair beside me I'd invented a half dozen exciting but unlikely possibilities.

"So," he said, "any ideas?"

I shrugged. "Not really, unless that paper you just submitted got rave reviews."

He grinned. "Very much more exciting than that. Roxanne has invited us to dive with great whites off Guadalupe Island."

"Um, excuse my ignorance, Brady, but I have no idea where that is."

"Guadalupe is a volcanic island about a hundred miles off the west coast of Mexico's Baja California Peninsula."

"A volcanic island a hundred miles out?"

He nodded. "You get there by dive boat, of course. And it's a chance to get amazingly close to great whites!"

Unsure what to say, I opened my mouth, shut it, and shook my head.

"What?" Brady asked.

"Um, diving with great white sharks? That doesn't sound real safe, Brady."

"We'd be in cages, of course."

I raised my eyebrows. "Well, that's a relief, I suppose."

He reached for my hand. "Mara, you've got to know that I wouldn't put you danger for anything, including a chance to see these sharks up close. We'd be doing what tourist divers routinely do, which is why Roxanne is interested. She wants to evaluate if the dives are as safe as advertised and truly an educational experience for the divers."

"So I assume the outfitters wouldn't know we are scientists," I said.

He nodded. "That's right. And Roxanne will help pay for trip for both of us."

"And when would we go?"

"It's the tail end of the dive season there, so next week."

"Next week," I repeated.

He took my hand and turned to look directly at me. "Of course, it's really short notice. I'm going for sure, but if you can't make it I'll be disappointed, naturally, but will understand."

Laughing, I shook my head. "I'll have to hoof it to get work done, but I'm not teaching this semester, there's nothing in my private life keeping me here now, and I can't remember the last time I took a vacation."

Grinning, he kissed me gently and whispered, "I'm so glad. So very, very glad."

After dinner we returned to the deck and watched the darkening sky morph from pink to crimson and finally to a fiery red as the sun dropped below the horizon.

I squeezed Brady's hand. "Okay, shark-watching tourism. I know absolutely nothing about it."

"Then you'll be surprised to learn how popular it is. Since the early nineties divers looking for adventure have spent millions to get close to all types of sharks. Globally, there's something like three hundred sites where divers observe sharks at close range. Roxanne's interest and mine is the resulting publicity in magazine articles and TV shows that help people understand sharks are beautiful animals threatened by over-fishing and certainly not man-eating monsters. We'd like to know if that message is getting through."

"Is whale-watching a good analogy?" I asked. "It's a billion-dollar tourist industry that's become very popular in the last, what, thirty years? These days, everyone loves whales, which certainly wasn't true in the past."

"It's been more than thirty years, Mara. People began watching whales off California in the fifties, but it really took off in New England when everyone wanted to see humpbacks breech, tail-slap, and all the rest. For sure, it's a hugely lucrative global industry. But shark-watching won't ever be that popular for obvious reasons."

"Because sharks, unlike humpbacks, are carnivores, and you've got to get under the water to shark-watch."

"Bingo," he said.

The next day I shared my news with three people who would care the most—well, two people and a lobster.

Phoning Angelo from my office, I gave him the condensed version of where Brady and I were going and why.

After a pause, Angelo said, "Let's see if I understand this correctly, Mara. You and Brady are going down to Baja Mexico to observe sharks from an island a hundred miles off the coast."

"That's right. It's a very popular thing divers do. We'll be on a boat, of course, and in those shark cages you've seen on television. It's all very safe."

After clearing his throat, Angelo asked, "Brady has done this, I take it?"

"Yes," I said, "and so has Roxanne, another scientist who organizes the dives as a kind of shark education program. She'll be with us. Brady and I can stop by and show you photos if you want."

"Naturally, I'd love to see both of you, Mara. But my looking at photos of this operation probably isn't a good idea. How about just dinner tomorrow night?"

After thanking Angelo for the invitation, I took the steps down to MOI's basement for a visit with Homer. As often happened, he emerged from hiding and crawled toward the front of his aquarium before I'd tapped on the glass.

Dropping some mussel meat into the aquarium, I said, "Hi, handsome."

Homer snatched the treat before it reached the bottom of his tank. As he picked the food apart with his leg pincers and passed small bits to his mouthparts, I told him about my upcoming trip. For the most part, he was more interested in the mussel than my adventure in Mexico, but he did pause for a moment when I first said "shark."

32

As I drove to Angelo's house for dinner the following night, it was a very good thing a deer didn't sprint across the road, because I probably would've hit it.

"Earth to Mara," Brady said.

"What?"

He cleared his throat. "I'll bet you have no idea what I've been talking about for the last few minutes."

Blinking, I scanned my memory. "Guilty as charged. Was it important?"

"I asked what you knew about Angelica."

"Angelica," I repeated. "Um, not a whole lot. She's been Angelo's, ah, partner for several months now. Let's see. She's Italian. I think she said she'd been a schoolteacher. That's about it."

"I see," he said. "Well, maybe we'll learn more tonight."

Angelo greeted us at the kitchen door before we had a chance to knock. "Come on in. Why don't you go into the living room while I tend to the marinara sauce? I'll join you in a couple of minutes."

Seated at one end of the couch, Angelica smiled and extended her hands as we walked in. "Mara and Brady, *buonasera*. How lovely to see you both."

While I settled onto the couch's other end, Brady accepted Angelica's brief hand squeeze before sitting next to me. Very much the gentleman, he patiently answered her questions, including where he was from and did he *really* study sharks and why.

Angelo joined us, sat next to Angelica on the couch, squeezed her hand, and said, "We've been talking about where in Italy Angelica's people are from—Elba."

"Elba," I repeated. "Napoleon's place of exile."

"*Molto triste*," she said. "So sad that people think of Napoleon first. Elba is a truly beautiful Tuscan island known for its clear, blue sea and lovely beaches." She looked at Brady. "They say scuba diving is very good there too."

"Huh," he said. "Elba sounds great all the way around."

"Speaking of scuba diving, tell us about this shark expedition in Mexico," Angelo said. "Baja, was it?"

Minimizing the danger as much as possible, Brady explained that we would be watching great white sharks from the safety of cages.

Angelo shook his head. "However you describe it, the whole thing sounds terrifying. Promise me, Brady, that you will take good care of Mara."

Brady reached over and held my hand. "Angelo, please understand that I would never, ever put Mara in harm's way. She's a treasure for both you and me."

On the drive home I asked Brady what he thought of Angelica.

"Actually, I liked her quite a bit. Her interest in my shark work seemed genuine, and it's obvious that she's crazy about Angelo. They make a pretty nice couple."

Listening to him, I realized the idea of Angelo and Angelica as a couple felt right and not threatening—and that understanding was an enormous relief.

Since neither of us was tired when we got home, I suggested we go into the living room for a "chat and herbal tea."

"Tea isn't my thing," Brady said. "But you go ahead."

Hot tea in hand, I settled onto the couch next to Brady. "Um, tell me about Guadalupe Island and shark diving."

He grinned. "I figured that's what you wanted to talk about."

I ignored the quip. "Sharks off Guadalupe. Why is diving to see them so terrific there?"

"Okay," he said. "First, a little about the island. Guadalupe is about a hundred fifty miles off Baja California's west coast. The cold California Current there is nutrient-rich, as you know."

I nodded. "And phytoplankton-rich as a result, which means there's an abundance of zooplankton and on up the food chain to animals like seals."

"That's right," Brady said. "Elephant seals, Guadalupe fur seals, and California sea lions. The fur seals are sitting ducks for sharks, so to speak, because they can't swim nearly as fast as the sea lions."

"So you've seen great whites go after the seals off Guadalupe?"

He nodded. "Yes, indeed. But I'll leave the gory details for another time, and we won't be seeing that."

I cleared my throat. "Okay, give me the details about diving with the sharks."

"We'll be cage-diving, not free-diving, Mara, from a good-sized oceangoing ship. Guadalupe is one of the best dive spots in the world because the water is so clear. You routinely see two or three Great Whites during a dive. To get a feel for the trip, why don't you check out the *Guadalupe Explorer*'s site on the web and read the guests' comments?"

Nodding, I said, "I'll do that for sure. Um, one last question. What kind of vessel is the *Guadalupe Explorer*?"

"She's an oceangoing steel ship. Roxanne tells me that both the crew and captain have commercial mariner qualifications. The ship meets the same safety requirements as large cruise ships."

"That sounds good. Speaking of Roxanne, where will we meet her?"

"The ship will be docked in Ensenada. It's south of Tijuana on the Baja Peninsula. We'll board there, and you might want to lose a few pounds before we go."

Draining the last of the tea, I put the cup onto the coffee table a little harder than I intended.

Stammering, Brady said, "You gotta know I was joking. I think your body...."

I laughed and held up my hand. "It's okay, Brady. I assume the food will be good on the ship?"

"Top chefs, apparently, the best of everything."

"How about the staterooms? What are they like?"

He shrugged. "Let's see. Good beds, our own shower, and enough room to be comfortable. Since we aren't paying customers, I assume our stateroom will be next to Roxanne's in the lowest deck."

"That's good. There's less chance to get seasick below decks. But we'll have to be careful about noise."

Brady tipped his head. "Noise?"

I reached for the teacup and stood. "You know, with Roxanne on the other side of the wall."

33

THE NEXT MORNING AFTER BREAKFAST BRADY GAVE ME more details about the trip.

"We'll fly from Boston directly to Ensenada, Mexico, via San Diego, stay two nights in Ensenada, and board the ship there."

"Stay where in Ensenada?"

"The Maria Vista Hotel. It's pretty nice, I promise."

"Um, I need to be clear about who is paying for what. This sounds pretty expensive."

He shrugged. "Well, like I said, the boat trip and shark cage diving won't cost us anything."

"Okay," I said. "But what about the flight and Maria whatever hotel?"

He looked to the side. "Um, there's something you should know about me."

Sipping my coffee, I eyed Brady across the top of my mug. "I don't like the sound of that."

"I'm not anything like an embezzler, if that's what you mean."

"Well that's a relief," I said. "So what, then, are you?"

"Rich."

"Rich," I repeated.

"I have, you know, a lot of money."

"Brady, there's nothing in the world wrong with that."

He shrugged but didn't say anything.

"If you don't mind my asking," I said, "how much money?"

"Mara, it's millions."

I blinked. "Millions as in more than a million?"

"Yeah, quite a bit more, although I can't tell you exactly."

I finished the coffee and slid the mug onto the table. "Brady, you have millions of dollars but aren't quite sure how much? What have you done with it?"

"I have a really nice house overlooking the ocean in Santa Cruz and an Aston Martin Lagonda. I give a lot to conservation agencies like the Sierra Club, the Nature Conservancy, and the Monterey Bay Aquarium. There's a good deal more left, but I really don't need anything."

"An Aston Martin and a Santa Cruz house right on the ocean," I repeated. "You were right. That's big-time money."

He looked to the side. "I hope you won't hold this against me. My grandfather made the money with shrewd investments. I just inherited it."

I nearly laughed but caught myself. The poor guy was dead serious.

"Don't be silly, Brady. Of course I won't. But I will let you pay for the hotel and the rest if that'll help you feel better."

"Great, that's settled then. As to the logistics, we'll need to fly out of Boston the day after tomorrow. It'll be pretty warm down in Mexico, so you don't need much in the way of clothing. You could bring your wetsuit if you want, but Roxanne said the ship has high-quality dive gear, including wetsuits. The water is quite warm down there, but as you know you'll still lose heat."

"Okay, Brady, all that sounds good. I can pack tonight."

"One last thing. Like I said, we'll fly from Boston. How do you usually get to Logan Airport from here?"

"There's a direct Portland bus to the airport. We'll have to take an early morning one, and I'll leave my car at the bus station parking lot."

"Bus," he repeated.

The quip was irresistible. "It's a form of transportation we poor folk use."

I spent the day tying up loose ends and letting people know where I was going and when I'd be back. In contrast to the department secretary, who said, "Have a nice trip," and returned to her work, Harvey was nonplussed.

We were sitting outside enjoying our lunch when I told her.

"Let me get this straight," she said. "You leave tomorrow for Mexico, spend a couple of days in a fancy hotel, take a ship to a volcanic island a hundred miles off Baja California, and cage-dive to watch sharks."

I nodded. "That's right."

"And Brady will pay for this."

"As Roxanne's guests on the dive boat we don't need to pay anything," I said. "But Brady will take care of the flights and hotel."

Grinning, she shook her head. "Well, you are one lucky girl, Mara. Hope you know that."

"It's all happened so fast I hardly know what to think. But of course, that's right. I am pretty darn lucky."

I spent the rest of the day taking care of paperwork I'd put off, responding to emails, and fielding phone calls. By the time I trudged up the stairs to Brady's office, it was nearly six p.m..

Seated behind his desk, he looked up and rubbed his eyes when I walked in.

"Looks like we've have the same kind of day," I said. "What do you say we catch a quick bite at the Lea Side and head home?"

Brady grinned. "When he worked, he really worked. But when he played, he really played."

"Um, I take it you are done with work and ready to play?"

His chair scraped the floor as he pushed it back and stood. "That was Dr. Seuss, if you didn't know. And yes, I'm very ready to play."

That evening, it only took me a half hour to pack my small duffle bag with a couple of bathing suits, T-shirts, shorts, jeans, underwear, nightclothes, toothbrush, shampoo, sunscreen, and my dive mask.

I carried the bag into the kitchen, where Brady was riffling through his own gear.

"Pretty sure I've got everything," I said.

He stood and stretched. "There's probably a decent store in the hotel, just in case. You might want to bring a dress, though."

"A dress," I repeated.

"He shrugged. "For the hotel restaurant. They might prohibit shorts. I'll bring a pair of kaki pants."

"No problem; I'll throw in a dress. Um, it'll he fun staying in a fancy hotel with you."

He walked up to me, lifted my chin, kissed me, and said, "Oh, yes. Very much fun indeed."

As it turned out, Brady's request that I pack a dress was just the beginning of a string of surprises.

34

THE BUS DROPPED US OFF AT THE AIRPORT TWO HOURS before our plane was scheduled to leave. Pulling my suitcase behind me, I followed Brady into the terminal and waited while he printed out our tickets.

He held up the tickets. "All set. Let's check the bags."

After I joined dozens of people waiting in a very long line, it took me a couple of minutes to realize that Brady wasn't behind me. Following the sound of his voice, I spotted him in the very much shorter first-class line. By the time I reached him, he was at the ticket counter speaking to the attendant. I didn't catch what they were talking about, but the woman must have said "sir" a half-dozen times.

Once we were through security I suggested we hang out in a restaurant for a while. "We've got a while before the plane leaves, and I know a good Italian place just up the concourse."

"Follow me," he said. "I've got a better idea."

With a shrug I followed him into an elevator that deposited us on the terminal's top floor. In contrast to the noise and bustle below, it was surprisingly quiet.

"Come on, Brady. Where the heck are you going?"

He pointed to a set of double doors. "There, and you'll see."

I followed him through the doors to a desk just inside. Brady reached for his wallet, pulled out a black card credit card, and handed it to the woman behind the desk. After a quick glance at the card, she said, "Welcome, Dr. MacFarlane. And this woman is your guest, I take it?"

He nodded. "That's right, Mara Tusconi, and we are on the next flight to San Diego."

She entered that information into her notebook, looked up with a smile, and said, "Enjoy your stay."

I followed Brady into a large lounge with comfy couches, stuffed chairs, and a handful of people reading, looking at their computers, drinking, and eating.

"Um, before we go further," I said, "tell me what this is."

He shrugged. "Pretend it's your own private club, which it is. There's all sorts of food and drink, but just ask if you want something in particular. We don't need to pay for any of it except alcohol. He nodded toward a room with large windows that overlooked the runway. "It'll be a little quieter back there, and we can watch the planes land and take off."

We'd barely found our seats when a woman walked over and asked what we'd like to drink.

Brady said, "I'll have a local microbrew," and looked at me.

"Um, sparkling water?"

"Will Perrier do?" the lady asked.

I nodded and watched as she scurried by a man carrying a white towel.

"You can take showers here?" I asked.

Brady shrugged. "Sure. I might take one myself before our flight. Airports always make me feel kind of grubby."

After we polished off some very tasty quiche, avocado caprese salad, and Ben & Jerry's chocolate chip ice cream, Brady left me alone to people watch while he showered. I checked out a few of the "guests" and tried to decide if they'd stand out in a crowd as especially wealthy. The couple sharing the closest couch wore jeans and T-shirts, so nothing ritzy there. Behind them, a guy staring out the window wore a tweed jacket with leather elbow patches, so I rated him as "rich." But the woman who frowned at her computer and twirled her hair was plebeian by my book.

Brady returned with damp hair and a dry towel for me. "Your turn, Mara, and you'll come back a new woman, take my word."

Doubting that, I accepted the towel with a smile, headed in the direction he'd just come from, and was assigned my private shower. The shower room was surprisingly large, sparkling clean, and well stocked with fancy soaps, shampoos, moisturizers, and lotions. Toasty warm and clean, I stepped out of the shower twenty minutes later, sampled a few of the lotions, and dressed.

Back in the lounge I fell into the chair next to Brady's.

"I *am* a new woman. Amazing what a difference that made!"

He beamed. "It's true. The good life is very, very good."

The next surprise came as we waited to board the plane. As usual, the first call for "people needing extra time" was followed by "first-class passengers only." And as usual, I waited with the crowd.

It took me a moment to realize that Brady had left my side and was about to hand our tickets to the flight attendant. He looked back, waved, and wiggled his eyebrows. For the very first time I was going to fly cross-country first-class.

35

WHILE BRADY STUFFED OUR CARRY-ON BAGS INTO AN overhead compartment, I settled into a window seat the size of a lounge chair. Brady was barely in his seat when the attendant asked what we'd like to drink and eat.

"We have roast beef or turkey sandwiches, quiche with salad, and white stilton cheese as an appetizer."

As she bustled off with our order for beer, wine, stilton, a sandwich, and quiche, I leaned closer to Brady and whispered, "The menu up here is a little different from the one in coach."

Grinning, he said, "And that's just the beginning. I bet you'll love it."

He was right, of course. It's amazing how quickly a six-hour flight passes when you can luxuriate in a seat that becomes a surprisingly comfy bed and are tucked in with a blanket, comforter, and real pillow.

I was nervous that we only had an hour in San Diego to make the flight down to Ensenada, but we boarded the tiny jet in plenty of time. As we approached, I realized that the Mexican city of Ensenada was larger and more built-up than I'd imagined. In the shadow of a large mountain range, the city hosted hundreds of pleasure boats, several luxury ocean liners, and a population of thousands.

Along with hundreds of Spanish-speakers, we moved quickly through security and customs and collected our bags.

"That went well," I said. "Now what?"

Brady pointed to an escalator. "Now we go outside to wait for the hotel bus. Get ready for some warmth and humidity."

Whenever I fly from cold-weather Maine to anywhere warm during the winter, the abrupt change in temperature always catches me by surprise. Pulling our suitcases behind us, we stepped out of the air-conditioned terminal into eighty-degree humidity.

At the hotel bus stop, I shrugged off the flannel shirt I'd been wearing and stuffed it into my suitcase. "Won't need this puppy for a while."

Brady pulled a wide-brimmed hat and sunglasses from his bag. "I've got sunscreen, Mara. Um, you might want to use it."

I held out one of my lily-white arms and grinned. "You think?"

When the van with a Maria Vista Hotel banner on its side pulled up, the driver jumped out and addressed Brady in rapid-fire Spanish. Much to my surprise, Brady responded in Spanish equally fast. I didn't understand a word of it.

Seated in the van on our way out of the airport, I reached over and squeezed Brady's hand. "I didn't know you were fluent in Spanish."

"California has the second-highest concentration of Spanish-speakers in our country, Mara. If you don't speak Spanish, you miss a great deal." He kissed my fingers. "Guess I have lots of talents you don't know about."

Once we reached the city, the van driver avoided the main streets and gave us a tour of "real" Ensenada. The narrow, crowded streets and shops with names like *panaderia* and *farmacia* reminded me of Havana, Cuba, which I'd visited a while back before restrictions complicated travel there.

Then, turning off the main road, the van passed through a guarded gate, between twin rows of tall coconut trees, and pulled to a stop at the entrance of what looked like a luxury Spanish villa with a red tile roof, cobble driveway, and bubbling fountain. As two men skipped down the stairs to open the van door and get our bags I turned to Brady and said, "Yes, this will certainly do."

Our top-floor room overlooked the beach, where waves splashed lazily across the sand. Directly below two empty swimming pools sparkled in the sun. Pulling aside sliding glass doors, I stepped out onto the deck, inhaled briny air warmed over the day, and listed to the rumble of the waves.

When Brady joined me, I took his hand. "I gotta say you've outdone yourself."

He nodded. "We've got two days alone here with nothing to do but enjoy ourselves. It's going to be a blast—an absolute blast."

Considering that I got up at five in the morning Eastern Time and Ensenada was three hours behind Maine, the first thing I enjoyed was a few hours of sleep.

Brady's voice cut through the haze of my siesta. "Mara, are you awake?"

I opened one eye. "I am now."

"Sorry. You've been asleep for three hours."

Blinking against the daylight, I sat up. "Three hours?"

"I thought you'd like to walk along the beach and maybe take a dip. It looks pretty nice out there."

We strolled hand in hand through water that slid up and back the gentle incline. "This is the softest sand I've ever walked through," I said. "Any idea why?"

"Far as I know, sand with round grains that's loosely packed feels soft. Run into the water if you want. I'll stay here with the soft sand."

I shook my head. "Let's head back. I'd love to take a shower and wash my hair."

36

CLEAN AND DECIDEDLY MORE PERKY, I JOINED BRADY on the deck where he was enjoying iced tea with a contented smile.

As I settled into the other chair, Brady lifted the bottle of sparkling water on the deck table. "Thought you'd like some water. It's easy to get dehydrated in this climate."

"Thanks. Is there a fridge in the room I missed?"

He shook his head. "Nope. Room service."

"Huh. Well, like I've said, it'll take me a while to get used to all this, ah, service."

Brady cleared his throat and looked out at the sea. "I hope you won't, you know, hold this against me."

For a moment, I thought he was joking, but the strain in his eyes said that he was not. I grasped his free hand. "Brady, I was joking. Of course I won't, as you said, hold this against you. How could I? And for your information, I'm having a blast."

He kissed my hand and nodded. "Well, that's good. Very, very good."

Freeing my hand, I reached for the seltzer, poured it into a glass on the table, and drained half the glass. "Perfect, and you're right. I'm more dehydrated than I knew."

He looked at his watch. "It's pushing five, Mara. Any thoughts on what you'd like to do about dinner?"

I shrugged. "Nothing big or fancy." Standing, I looked down at the pool and expansive deck with tables shaded by several pergolas and oversized umbrellas. "It looks like they serve food down there. That'd be easy."

It was still on the warm side at seven in the evening, and the large umbrellas provided welcome shade. The menu was written in English on one side and Spanish on the other. Since my Spanish was essentially nonexistent, I scanned the English version. Brady, I noticed, chose Spanish.

"The tuna minilla empanadas look good," I said. "What's not to like about tuna, tomatoes, olives, raisins, and olives wrapped in a puffy pastry?"

With a "hmm," he continued to examine the menu. When the waiter came by to take our order, Brady chatted with him in rapid-fire Spanish.

As the waiter left, I said, "Brady, that's impressive."

He shrugged. "Not really. Lots of Anglos in California speak Spanish."

"By the way, what did you ask him?"

"If the tuna was fresh, which it is."

"Oh, thanks. You know, a girl could get used to this."

He winked. "I hope so. Um, your parents must have taken you on vacations, so where did you go and what did you do?"

"Sure. We went camping at Acadia National Park and a few other places we could drive to in New England. They bought a Boston Whaler so we could see some of Maine's islands and camp out there. There are literally thousands of islands off the Maine coast."

"Sounds terrific," he said.

"Okay, Brady, I've told you a little about my parents but know nothing about yours."

He nodded. "You'd like them, I think. My Mom's name is Katherine, but people call her Kate. Dad's name is Henry. Dad's father had money smarts and made a ton of it with Tampax."

That took me aback for a moment. "As in tampons?"

"Yup. My grandfather was was a gynecologist who realized that lots of women would really go for Tampax. He invested early and big, and it really paid off."

"So that's where you money comes from. What are they like, your parents?"

Thinking, he looked to the side. "Very outdoorsy, but they don't do much camping. Yachting is more their speed, along with downhill skiing. They love to travel and have gone all over the world together—Europe, of course, but also South America, Australia, New Zealand, Antarctica, Africa, the Middle East."

"And they live in California?"

"Malibu."

"Whoa," I said. "Expensive, gorgeous, and right on the Pacific Ocean."

"Yeah, all three. It's where I got psyched about marine animals like California gray whales. Their entire population migrates just off the Malibu coast every winter and spring."

"Brady, that sounds amazing. What about great white sharks?"

"My parents took me on a whale- and shark-watching boat trip, and we sure saw sharks. Everyone else, including Mom and Dad, jumped back when sharks got close to the boat, but I leaned over the side to get a better look. Mom nearly fainted."

"I can imagine," I said. "Brady the shark whisperer."

37

THE NEXT DAY WAS MELLOW AND UNEVENTFUL—UNTIL IT wasn't. After breakfast, we lazily walked up and back along the beach and stopped to watch some very talented surfers paddle their boards.

"Surfing 101, Brady. I know zero about the sport."

"Sure. The concept of surfing is simple, but in practice it isn't. As you can see, these guys paddle out to the surf line, sit on their boards, and just watch the waves."

"What's a surf line, and what are they watching for?"

"Where the waves break, and a surfer tries to determine if a wave is strong enough to ride but not so strong that it'll toss him when it breaks."

"Okay, the surfer is at the surf line and sees a wave he can ride. Then what?"

"At that point he'll paddle quickly to catch the rising wave. Just as it breaks, he jumps from his belly to his feet and crouches on the board. He can stand up if he's an experienced surfer. Then he rides the wave as it breaks toward the shore."

Squinting, I watched one of surfers. "That guy didn't come all the way in to shore."

"When the waves lose power, they turn their boards back toward open water and do it all over again."

"An excellent surfing lesson, Brady. Thanks."

Pointing, he said, "Hold it a minute, Mara. Look straight ahead beyond the surf line. I'm pretty sure I saw a dorsal fin sticking out of the water."

Squinting, I shaded my eyes with my hand and was about to tease Brady that he had an overactive imagination when I spotted the fin.

"Good lord, Brady, there's a surfer lying on his board paddling right toward the shark! Quick, let's alert the lifeguards. That guy's in serious danger!"

We sprinted to the lifeguard tower to alert whoever was on duty. Seated beneath a beach umbrella atop the wooden structure, an exceedingly tan twenty-something guy squinted down at us while Brady told him what we'd seen in rapid-fire Spanish. For a moment, it seemed as if he didn't believe us, but after he picked up his binoculars and fixed on the spot where Brady was pointing he jumped into action.

The shark alarm was loud, piercing, and did the job. Surfers out on the water squatted on their boards, lay on their bellies, and paddled quickly toward shore. The handful of people who'd been bobbing and splashing in the shallow water stumbled out onto the beach. The lifeguard and another guy pushed a two-person jet ski into the water and zoomed out to the oblivious surfer.

Watching it all unfold through the binocs was bad enough, but hearing the surfer's screams was absolutely terrifying.

I grabbed Brady's arm and handed him the field glasses. "Good lord, the shark must've attacked that guy."

Brady adjusted the optics and gave me a running narrative. "The lifeguards just reached the surfer, and I don't see the shark fin. Um, the guy is lying on his surfboard and it looks like there's blood floating on the water surface. The lifeguards are leaning over the side of their jet ski. I can't really tell what they are doing, but the surfer is still on his board. Wait, the lifeguards have tied a line to the surfboard. I think they'll try to tow the board to shore with the surfer still on it. Yes, that's what they're doing."

Behind us, the loud, high-pitched sound of an ambulance got louder and louder. Moments later, uniformed medics sprinted across the sand to the water's edge. Slowly towing the surfboat and injured surfer, the lifeguard boat reached shallow water, and two medics waded into the water to steady the surfboard and examine the injured man.

I squeezed Brady's arm. "Can you understand what the medics are saying?"

"*Mucha perdida de sangre de su brazo,*" he said. "Lots of blood loss from his arm. I'm guessing the shark bit the guy in the arm when he was paddling out to deeper water."

Brady and I strode up and down the beach for a while before I felt anything like my normal self. A half-hour into the walk, Brady asked if I wanted to talk about what happened or would rather not.

"Good question," I said. "Since I can't stop thinking about it, talking would be good. Let's see. If you hadn't seen that fin, this might've been even more of a disaster."

He nodded. "You got that right. If we hadn't decided to take a walk when we did, that surfer would probably be dead now."

"He'll pull through, don't you think?"

Brady shrugged. "That depends on how much damage the shark did to his arm. At the very least, that guy won't be playing the piano for a while."

Later, when things had calmed down, we asked the lifeguard about the frequency of shark attacks as he added gasoline to the jet ski. His English was good, so I could understand him.

"The sharks, they are here," he said, "which is why we have the danger signs. But some people ignore the signs, so if someone swims too far out, we use the jet ski to tell them it's too dangerous. Most of the time they come right in, but not always."

"Has anyone died from a shark attack here?" I asked.

"Not here, *gracias a Dios*. But yes, in other places in Mexico."

38

DECIDING NOT TO SWIM IN THE OCEAN, BRADY AND I splashed around in the pool for a while and went up to our room to shower and "chill," as Brady put it.

We had dinner in the hotel restaurant and talked about logistics for the next day.

"The hotel shuttle will drop us off at the Ensenada dock where the locals keep their boats. That's away from the huge luxury liners. Roxanne spent last night on the *Guadalupe Explorer* and said the ship will pick us up at the dock."

"Got it," I said. "You were right about us taking a couple of days to unwind before we boarded the ship. Flying cross-country and immediately stepping onto that ship would've been hard, especially since, um, I get seasick."

He smirked. "You, an oceanographer, get seasick?"

"Don't worry, I packed my medication. And once I'm out there for a day or two I'm fine, unless we hit a hurricane or something."

"Mara, I do have a serious question. Have you even gotten seasick on scuba?"

"Thank goodness, no. Under the water I'm fine. It's the ship, you know, rocking back and forth that does me in, especially if I'm in a stuffy room or something like that."

The hotel shuttle left us at the Ensenada dock as the *Guadalupe Explorer* rounded a jetty and steamed in our direction. Just as Brady had said, she was very much an ocean-going ship a good two hundred feet long with ample aft deck space for divers preparing for entry into the water, large wraparound windows, and a shaded top-deck with patio chairs.

I pointed to a round structure on the upper deck. "What's that?"

"A hot tub for divers coming out of the water, which feels amazingly nice."

"I can only imagine."

As the ship pulled alongside the dock, a deckhand jumped onto the pier to get our bags while two more helped us step aboard and said, "*Bienvenida a* Guadalupe Explorer."

Roxanne waved from the upper deck and then hurried down to meet us. "Can you believe it? Here we are on this amazing ship heading out to watch sharks! Come on, I'll give you a tour."

As the ship left the harbor, Roxanne showed us around the *Guadalupe Explorer*, which turned out to be quite a bit more impressive than I'd envisaged. Our first stop was the upper aft deck.

"Up here's where we get ready for our dives," Roxanne said. "There's plenty of room for us and our gear, as you can see. I can tell you that the ship's dive equipment is top rate. She nodded toward the hot tub. "As you know, even in Caribbean water divers can get plenty cold. That hot tub's pretty nice."

She pointed to a set of glass doors. "In there's where we have our meals."

Large and luxurious, the dining room held twenty-odd tables covered in white linen. Roxanne pointed to the other end of the room. "The bar is back there. It's free, whatever you want."

Laughing, I shook my head. "Looks like I better watch what I eat!"

"Don't you know it," she said. "It's pretty hard to say no to ginger layer cake with cream cheese frosting, chocolate-covered strawberry cheesecake, blueberry trifle, and pecan pie."

"So is it buffet style?" I asked.

She shook her head. "Oh, no. They serve us at the table."

Beyond the dining room was a large, comfortable space with couches, lounge chairs, coffee tables, a small library of books and magazines, and another bar.

"The lounge is where we hang out before dinner to talk about the dive schedule, what we saw during a dive, that kind of thing," Roxanne said. "Next, I'll take you down to your room. As you know, we are in the lower deck."

"That's just fine with me," I said. "It's more stable and quieter."

Brady and I followed Roxanne down three sets of stairs to the rooms belowdecks. When we reached the end room, she handed two keys to Brady. "Here you are, and I'm next door. Your bags are already inside. Why don't you get settled and then look for me in the lounge next to the dining room where the captain will welcome us and go over logistics? Lunch will be right after that."

Brady opened the door with his key, and we stepped into a room that, again, was larger than I'd imagined. A double bed took up much of the space, but there was ample room for a coffee table, good-sized closet, and two chairs. I stuck my head into the bathroom, where there was a regular-size shower stall, I was happy to see, plus a pile of fluffy towels and the usual lineup of shampoo, creams, soaps, and toothpaste. On the door hung two white terrycloth bathrobes.

Hands under his head, Brady lay on the bed. "So what do you think?"

"It's terrific. The only thing missing is a large window with a view."

Brady turned to look at our porthole. "Guess that'll have to do."

I peered through the porthole and watched a school of fish swim by. "We won't get any sunlight down here, but the underwater show will make up for that."

39

CAPTAIN SULLIVAN WAS FORTYISH, DEEPLY TANNED, experienced, and funny. He began with an explanation that Guadalupe Island was one of the best places in the world to watch sharks.

"Only Guadalupe Island can boast shark viewing in beautiful clear blue water with a hundred foot–plus visibility," he said. "We've identified over three hundred unique great white sharks in the bay where we stage our submersible shark cage diving operations. Our cages give you an authentic shark encounter experience down thirty feet where the sharks naturally spend their time. That means we don't use chum—that's fish parts, bones, and blood—because the sharks are already there."

"Without chum, these great whites are more relaxed and curious, and they come in *much* closer to the cages," he said. "Believe me, it's an unforgettable rush when a great white eyes you from fifty feet away and then swims over for a closer look."

I scanned the room to get an idea of people's reactions to the "unforgettable rush" awaiting them. Many were nodding, but a group of women in the back looked startled and, I assumed, were wondering what the heck they'd gotten themselves into.

"As to regulations," Sullivan continued, "the Mexican Park Service requires you to stay in the cages at all times, including keeping your arms, hands, and cameras inside. And please don't pollute the beautiful clear blue waters of Guadalupe with suntan lotion or any other contaminants.

"One of our divemasters will be with you on all dives for your safety and to increase your chances of shark sightings. You should be ready and dressed in your wetsuit ten minutes before your scheduled cage time. A wetsuit is usually adequate to keep you warm, but we do have hoods and extra gloves available. Once more, see any of our divemasters for assistance.

"For your safety, all diving is done using a hookah system—otherwise known as surface-supplied air—and our cages designed to provide maximum protection for you *and* for our sharks. It is absolutely vital that the sharks are never negatively affected or injured during their interaction with us.

"As to logistics, today is a day of travel and relaxation. Tomorrow there will be an orientation briefing in the morning, followed by a mandatory fire safety drill. Our "Introduction to Sharks" presentation is this afternoon, followed by a chance to try out a shark cage on the back deck and surface of the water, and then cocktails at nineteen-hundred, seven in the evening.

"We like to arrive at here at the island early in the evening so that guests can enjoy dinner in a nice, calm, protected anchorage and have a peaceful snooze before the excitement of diving first thing the next morning.

"Finally, the logistics of our shark trips are pretty straight-forward. We open the cages after breakfast and close them before dinner. Divemasters are either in the water or on the dive deck. We have enough cages in the water to provide virtually unlimited diving in our surface cages and least three dives a day in submersible cages for certified divers."

Sullivan ended the presentation by thanking us again for choosing *Guadalupe Explorer*, encouraging anyone to approach him with questions or comments, and apologizing for a first-night dinner that the cooks had little time to prepare.

Over before-dinner "cocktails"—local beer for Brady and wine for me and Roxanne—we agreed that the captain's presentation was very good.

"It's not easy giving that kind of talk to a mixed crowd like this," Roxanne said. "I think he balanced overview with just enough detail."

"I agree," Brady said. "Tomorrow evening I'll ask him to describe seasonal differences in the sharks they see. Things like males versus females, or older sharks versus younger ones."

Roxanne nodded. "But remember, you've got to sound like an average Joe."

"I never thought about this before," I said, "but what, exactly is an average Joe?"

She shrugged. "You know, ordinary Joe, Joe Sixpack, Joe Schmo. For females it'd be ordinary Jane, plain Jane."

"You see a lot of average Joes on TV," Brady said. "Think Homer Simpson and Archie Bunker, but off the top of my head I can't think of a television plain Jane."

Pulling a chair closer, a pushy guy with buck teeth and a shrill voice interrupted our discussion. "Hey, did I hear Homer Simpson? He's my big-time hero. By the way, I'm Felix Friendly. I'm sure you've read my stories about why your brain thinks shopping is as good as sex and dogs can read our minds in *Screwball Science* magazine?"

Since Roxanne and Brady looked at each other and shrugged, it was obvious they had no idea who Felix was. Unfortunately, though, I did.

Aware that I couldn't broadcast my profession, I soft-pedaled my response. "Wasn't there a controversy about the dog piece? Let's see, something about the scientific research being distorted?"

Felix's eyes narrowed. "Scientists drive me nuts. You'd think they'd appreciate the publicity, wouldn't you? But no. They just whine that a dog intuiting human emotions is very different from reading people's minds."

When it was obvious that I didn't agree with him Felix left to find, I assumed, more gullible guests to prey upon.

Checking to make sure he was out of earshot, I leaned closer to Roxanne and Brady. "I wouldn't trust that guy with a bucket of water if my knickers were on fire."

Grinning, Brady repeated, "Knickers?"

"You know," I said, "briefs, boxers, butt-huggers, tighty-whities."

Roxanne stood. "Hate to break off this enlightening discussion, but they've opened the dining room doors and people are filing in."

As the captain had explained, dinner was buffet-style this first evening. He had sounded apologetic, but the roast turkey with stuffing, roast beef, salmon in lemon sauce, steamed potatoes, asparagus with toasted almonds and lemon, Waldorf salad, and hot rolls, plus ginger layer cake, chocolate-covered cheesecake, and lemon blueberry trifle were first rate.

After dinner, Roxanne explained she was exhausted after the cross-country flight, wished us both "shark-filled sweet dreams," and left.

"How about we go up to the top deck?" I said. "It'd be nice to watch the sun go down from there."

We had the upper deck to ourselves, including an area not covered by the canopy and open to the sky. At anchor and bobbing gently with the waves, our ship had reached her destination. In the distance, a dark and steep-sided Guadalupe Island looked like the ancient volcano it was. Turning, I sucked in a breath as the fiery-red sun slipped down into sea on the horizon.

"You won't believe this, Mara. Turn around," Brady said.

Pulling myself away from the sun's spectacle, I looked in the opposite direction and gasped. An enormous alabaster full moon was rising up out of the water.

"Brady, make a wish," I whispered.

Wrapping his arms around my shoulders, he pulled me to him. "How can I wish for anything better than this?"

40

AFTER BREAKFAST, THE CAPTAIN AGAIN REVIEWED THE day's itinerary—fire drill and introduction to the cages on deck followed by surface-water cage dives for interested guests. "The cages hold two guests and a divemaster. That limits how many dives you'll do in a day, but I think you'll find several forty-five-minute dives tiring because you get pretty cold even in wetsuits."

As instructed, Brady and I returned to the cabin, found our orange life jackets in a closet drawer, put them on, memorized our fire station, and waited for the fire drill alarm.

In the thirty seconds it took for Brady to secure his life jacket I'd barely figured out how to put the thing on. "These things are always too big for me," I complained, "and there's always a strap left over I don't know what to do with."

"I'll help you," he said, "but don't squirm around."

He pulled the last strap tightly around my waist when the piercing sound of the fire alarm rang through the ship. As a crewmember yelled, "Fire! Fire!" above us, we walked quickly along the corridor, up the stairs, and out onto the aft deck to our station—the rescue boat. We waited there with a half-dozen life-jacket-clad guests until the all clear signal was given, trooped back to the cabin, shed the life jackets, and returned to the deck to hear the do's and don'ts of cage diving.

Ann, the divemaster assigned to Brady and me, started with the do's—what we should do. "You'll breath air from above through a hookah hose, so do keep the hose in your mouth at all times." She grinned. "I know that sounds obvious, but you'd be surprised how many people try to talk underwater, which causes them to gag. Also, never put your hands or feet outside the cage. Sharks are smart, curious animals, and you sure don't want them to get interested in any part of your body. Don't bang anything against the cage, because that might attract a shark as well. Finally, if, for any reason, you need to surface, don't hesitate to signal me by pointing up and moving your hand up and down a bit. We don't want anyone to have a panic attack underwater, feel nauseous, or anything else."

Ann asked if we had any "underwater experience" and seemed pleased that we were scuba-certified and had never run into any difficulty.

"It's a lot easier to go down with folks who know what they are doing," she said. "Maybe later I'll entertain you with some of the nutty things people have tried. Let's get you outfitted in your wetsuits, and then you are good to go. First dive is at fifteen hundred; that's three this afternoon. Be suited up at least ten minutes before that. Also, I'd recommend a light lunch."

"I've got a quick question, before we go," I said. "Do you folks attract the sharks toward the cage?"

Ann nodded. "Right, I forgot to mention that. Once we are underwater, a crewmember may toss a smallish bag on a line into the water if the sharks are down deep. The bag contains fish, which brings the sharks closer."

Seated at our assigned table with Roxanne and five other guests, I picked at my Waldorf salad.

"Anything wrong with the lunch?" Roxanne asked.

I shook my head. "Not a bit. It's usually one of my favorites, but I'm just not hungry."

"I'd be surprised if you weren't a little nervous," she said. "After all, you'll be underwater with a huge carnivore that's usually pretty docile but sometimes isn't."

Unsure whether she was joking, I stared at her.

She shrugged. "Sorry, I don't mean to make light of this. You'll be fine. We all will. Shark tourism is incredibly popular, and that wouldn't be the case if people got hurt."

At two-thirty Brady and I had wiggled into our wetsuits and pulled on our gloves and booties. It was time for a hookah lesson.

"Hookah basics," Ann said. "In hookah diving, an air compressor delivers air through a long hose called a down-line to the diver underwater. Our compressor will be up on the ship. The hoses are made of bright-colored vinyl plastic that doesn't kink and is positively buoyant so it doesn't tangle. As with scuba, holding your breath can result in injury because your lungs expand as you ascend. So don't hold your breath as we go back up. And also like scuba, you slowly must exhale while we ascend, or air bubbles can block your blood vessels. Watch me and do the same. The deepest we'll go is thirty feet, but as you know that's deep enough to cause problems."

"Finally," she said, "we'll have a scuba tank with us in case the hooka gets blocked for some reason. That's never happened to me, but you've got to be prepared for anything."

"I'm unclear how we get into the cage before we go down," I said.

She nodded. "Yes, I was just getting to that. We climb in when the cage is over the side of the ship but still out of the water. As you can see, there's an entrance on the top of the cage that leads to a little ladder inside the cage. So, are you folks ready to go get into the cage and see sharks?"

41

ANN CLIMBED BACKWARDS DOWN THE LADDER, STEPPED TO the side, and watched until we were standing next to her. Holding one of the hookah hoses, she reviewed the basics of its use, and reminded us to keep our hands and feet inside the cage.

I secured my dive mask, put the hookah hose in my mouth, and slowly breathed compressed air as Ann watched.

"All right," she said. "Are we good to go down and see sharks up close?"

After Brady and I gave her a thumbs up, I held onto one of the cage's thick metal bars and looked down into the water. Thirty-odd feet below, dim shadows of an ancient marine creature unsettled me. Like it or not, I was about to be up close and personal with a fifteen-foot carnivore.

As we sank beneath the surface, I was amazed by the clarity of the water. With visibility exceeding fifty feet, I could see schools of little blue, silver, and yellow fish dashing this way and that. Ann touched my arm and pointed to an impressively large green sea turtle gliding beneath us. Ten feet down, Ann paused the descent, checked once more to make sure we were okay, and gave the go-ahead signal to the deckhands above.

I felt surprisingly calm as we came closer and closer to the sharks gliding below us. I knew, of course, that great whites had conveyor belts of upper and lower extremely sharp teeth designed to rip apart big chunks of flesh. Still, it was hard to believe that these gently meandering giants wanted to cause us harm.

At thirty feet, Ann stopped our descent and signaled that we'd wait there. The two closest sharks circling below appeared not to notice us at all. I assumed the appearance of strange creatures from above behind thick metal bars was something they'd seen dozens of times. For quite a while—ten minutes at least—I was mesmerized by the graceful back-and-forth sweep of their powerful tails as the sharks circled beneath us. Great whites were indeed amazing and beautiful animals, graceful as any bird and mysterious as any creatures on earth. It was stunning that this remarkable creature was under threat by humans, simply for the purpose of making soup.

I also realized the great whites weren't just white. Instead, only their underbellies were white, while their upper bodies were dark. Looking down, I understood the genius of this design. From above where I was, their gray coloring was effective camouflage and the sharks were difficult to see against the dark shadows of the ocean bottom. From below, in contrast, a white creature would blend in with the sunlit surface.

All too soon, Ann signaled the ship's crew that we were ready to ascend. Back on deck she asked for our first impressions.

I'd pulled off my hood and mask and wiped salt water from my eyes. Blinking, I shook my head. "It's indescribable. A giant carnivore sweeping back and forth below us so gracefully, just minding its own business."

She grinned. "We can do another dive before dinner at five if you folks are up for it."

I looked at Brady, who raised his eyebrows, which I took as a yes. So a few hours later, we climbed down the ladder into the cage again and began our descent.

This time the sharks were farther away than before—distant circling shadows a good deal deeper than we wanted to go. Given that situation, Ann had explained earlier that deckhands on the ship would draw them closer with small bags of fish parts they dragged through the water. It took a couple of tosses before the sharks appeared to notice the bait, but they headed up in our direction when they did.

One shark very nearly snapped a bag off its line before the crewmate noticed and yanked the bag up and out of the water. Seemingly agitated, the shark swam quick circles where the bag had been, dove down, came back up, and repeated the maneuver a few more times. That's when, as they say, all hell broke loose.

Someone, by mistake we later assumed, threw a piece of what looked very much like bologna into the water—a big piece of oily, smelly, greasy bologna. Made of pork fat, the meat was a shark magnet. That would have been okay if the sausage meat sank directly down into the shark's mouth, but it didn't.

Instead, the bologna, swinging back and forth in the water, drifted closer and closer to our cage. And well aware of the danger, Ann saw what was happening but was helpless to do anything about it. Fascinated, I suddenly realized I was mesmerized by a piece of smoked sausage named after an Italian city. The insight struck me as so absurd I was overcome by a fit of the giggles— definitely not appropriate given my underwater location.

42

IS HAND ON MY SHOULDER, BRADY TIPPED HIS HEAD and gave me an "are you okay?" look. Unable to speak with the hookah in my mouth, I mimed the back-and-forth swing of the meat slice, but Brady merely shrugged.

The bologna continued to drift toward us, shifted up with the current, and finally landed on a bottom strut of our cage, where it stayed.

As we stared at the slice, it was obvious that neither Ann, Brady, or I had any idea what to do. If we tried to slide the meat off the strut, we'd release shark-attracting fats into the water. On the other hand, leaving the bologna in place could draw sharks toward us as well.

Ann signaled the crew on deck that we wanted to ascend, and quickly. A moment later an alpha great white rose up from below and clamped its powerful jaws on a bottom strut. Jumping closer to Brady, I got an up close and personal look at the shark's serrated bladelike and absolutely terrifying teeth.

After a quick shudder, the cage finally began to ascend, but the stubborn shark hung on until we broke though the surface. Staring down into the water, I watched a dark shadow circle until it disappeared.

Back on deck, I asked Brady and Ann to wait until we were alone and said, "I don't think what happened was an accident. Someone intentionally threw that piece of meat into the water."

Ann frowned and said, "But why would anyone want to do such a thing?"

I shook my head. "Who knows, but I'm damned well going to find out."

After we'd showered and changed, Brady and I sat in our room and talked about what happened.

"I certainly agree that a single piece of bologna is very unlikely to float into our cage by itself," he said, "but why would anyone want to do that?"

"Who knows? There are lots of crazies out there, including eco-activists who might see all this as shark exploitation and want to scare people off. Unfortunately they won't be wearing *Save the Sharks* T-shirts so we know who they are.

"That's right," he said. "But we can pay attention to what guests say. Somebody might give themselves away."

Nodding, I agreed. "Look, why don't I go up to the lounge alone, sip wine, flip through some magazines, and eavesdrop?"

"Okay," he agreed. "But we don't know what we are dealing with, so be careful."

The lounge was empty when I carried my glass of wine to a two-person couch toward the back and picked up *California Outdoors* magazine. A couple of minutes later two thirtyish women walked in and ordered an "eco-friendly craft beer."

"We have Salmon River Brewery," the bartender said. "Will that do?"

With a shrug, one of the women said, "I guess so." Then, beer in hand, she walked over to a coffee table and put her glass on it. As she turned around to pull a chair closer to the table I could clearly see that the back of her T-shirt read *Solo Earth.*

Back in our stateroom I told Brady about the T-shirt.

He shrugged. "So, she's a Solo Earther. That doesn't make her dangerous."

"Come on, Brady. The Solo Earth nuts are one of the most radical environmental groups in the country. They do things like chain themselves to trees in old-growth forests so they aren't felled. Tossing a piece of bologna overboard so it floats onto a shark cage would be nothing to them. We've got to report this to Captain Sullivan so he and his crew make sure it doesn't happen again."

Grateful for the information, Sullivan said, "Thank so you very much for bringing this to my attention. Throwing a piece of meat overboard near a submerged shark cage is an outrageous, very dangerous thing to do. The crew will be informed, and I'll double the number of crewmembers on deck during the dives to make sure it doesn't happen again."

That evening waiters served us a lovely dinner—salmon with roasted potatoes—which I picked at while Brady entertained everyone seated at our table with a sanitized version of "the shark-bologna adventure." The group especially appreciated our description of the swinging slice of sausage as it wafted its way toward our cage.

Looking concerned, Millie from Chicago asked, "But weren't you frightened?"

"It happened so fast," Brady answered. "And, you know, sharks are such amazing, beautiful animals."

Assuming I interpreted Millie's stare correctly, "amazing" and "beautiful" were not descriptions of sharks that she was used to hearing.

As Brady launched into a detailed description of a shark's olfactory organs inside nostril-like holes called nares, I kicked him gently in the shin. He'd forgotten that we were tourists like everyone else, not marine scientists.

Frowning, Millie said, "You sure know a lot about sharks, don't you?"

Brady shrugged. "Ah, I'm a real fan of that *Shark Tank* TV show, and I've read a lot of stuff."

After dinner Roxanne, Brady, and I climbed the stairs to the upper deck where we could enjoy the sunset. As we watched the pink horizon turn fuchsia, Roxanne congratulated Brady on his response to Millie. "*Shark Tank* on television, that was quick thinking," she said.

"It was," I agreed. "Does the show exist?"

"Indeed it does," he said. "But it's about people pitching ideas to investors."

Over the next two uneventful days we followed the same routine—breakfast, cage dive, hot tub, nap; lunch, cage dive, hot tub, nap; before-dinner drinks, dinner, bed. We completed our final cage dive on the morning of the third day, warmed up in the hot tub, and ate lunch as the *Guadalupe Explorer* turned back toward Ensenada. On the town dock we thanked Roxanne for an amazing trip and promised we'd share our photos and keep in touch.

As Roxanne headed for her hotel to "pack and get my act together," Brady and I walked in the other direction.

"I wasn't just saying that, you know," I said. "That truly was the trip of a lifetime."

Nodding, Brady said, "And a thousand times better because you were there."

I squeezed his hand. "Brady, that's sweet. So what's the itinerary now? San Diego and then Boston?"

"Could you possibly take another few days before we go back? I'd love to fly up to Santa Cruz. We'd stay at my house and maybe you'd meet my parents."

43

HAVING NEVER BEEN TO SANTA CRUZ, I ANTICIPATED California ritz, but I couldn't have been more wrong. Brady's home was charming, with weathered wood, two bedrooms separated by a sizable living room, and large sliding glass doors that opened to a deck and stairs down to the beach.

We arrived in the early afternoon, enjoyed a barefoot walk along the beach, splashed through shallow water, and returned to the deck for lunch and cold drinks.

Swirling my iced tea, I said, "The turkey and cheese sandwiches were excellent, and there's all sorts of food and drink in the fridge. How'd you manage that?"

He shrugged. "A guy named Marco takes care of the house and shops for me."

"Well, next time you see Marco tell him he's got great taste."

Brady's phone pinged and he scrolled through a couple of messages. "My parents want to know if we'd like to meet them for dinner in town this evening."

"Of course," I said. "But nothing fancy. I've just got my clothes from the boat trip."

"No worries, Mara. My parents like things casual."

I nodded. "Good. Um, what should I call them?"

"Kate and Henry. Definitely not Mr. and Mrs. MacFarlane."

The maître d in Brady's favorite Santa Cruz Mexican restaurant welcomed him as an old friend.

"Ah, señor Brady, I've missed you. Your parents are already here. *Buen provecho*."

A gray-haired version of Brady waved at us from the back of the restaurant stood and as we approached. After he hugged Brady, Henry reached for my hand and shook it.

"Kate and I are so very pleased to meet you, Mara. I understand that you two have just come from a thrilling adventure. Please come, sit down, and tell us all about it."

An hour later it was hard to believe I hadn't known Kate and Henry for decades. They appreciated the absurdity and danger of the "bologna event," wanted to know about MOI's history and the people who work there, and seemed genuinely interested in the nature of my research, including my recent trip to the Sargasso Sea.

"An astounding place, the Sargasso," Henry said. "The center of a huge whirlpool created by currents plus *Sargassum*, a seaweed found nowhere else in the world and home to a fish that mimics the weed it inhabits."

"Exactly right," I agreed. "On the trip I was able to scuba dive around and beneath the *Sargassum*, and that helped me realize how amazingly well camouflaged those little fish are. Sometimes, my nose was right up to the seaweed, and I still couldn't see them."

"When will you two head back to Maine?" Kate asked.

"The day after tomorrow," Brady said. "We fly out of San Diego."

Henry frowned. "But what about the hurricane?"

"What hurricane?" Brady and I said in unison.

"Well, you better check when you get home. There's a big storm heading north along the east coast."

An hour later we tuned into the weather channel to learn the bad news. Jolene, a Category 2 storm, promised to cause "extensive rain and extremely dangerous winds."

Brady shook his head. "The airlines will shut down on the east coast for a couple of days. We'll have to wait until things improve."

"Well, that's a bummer," I said.

He shrugged. "How about we turn this into something positive?"

"Such as?"

"Well, have you ever been to Baja? The ecology is amazing."

"I know species diversity is very high there," I said, "but that's about it."

Brady nodded. "The Baja Peninsula is one of the largest protected areas in Mexico. It's home to something like five-hundred plant species, and about a quarter of those are seen nowhere else. There are also endemic animals like black jackrabbits and the Baja California rattlesnake."

"Think I'll miss the rattlesnake," I said, "but it'd be amazing to see a black jackrabbit."

An hour later Brady had rescheduled our flights so we'd leave the following afternoon for Baja and fly to Boston two days after that.

"And I found a great place for us to stay in Baja," he said. "It's nice but not fancy, and they offer ecology excursions."

Our plans made, we decided to take an evening stroll down the deserted beach in the twilight. Barefoot, we splashed through wet sand as the waves washed up and back.

Suddenly, Brady stopped and turned toward me. "There's something I need to ask you, Mara."

"The last time someone said that to me, the outcome wasn't good," I teased.

Deadly serious, Brady took my hands in his, and knelt down on one knee. "Mara Tusconi, will you marry me?"

I was gobsmacked but recovered quickly. "I, um…that is… Brady, of course I'll marry you!"

Brady fumbled in one of his pockets, brought out a ring, and slid it onto my left ring finger. Even in the dim light the diamonds sparkled.

I held out my hand. "Brady, this is an absolutely gorgeous ring."

"It's my grandmother's ring on my mother's side. Mom gave it to me last night."

"When we were at dinner?"

"Um, when you went to the bathroom."

For some reason, the image of Kate slipping Brady an engagement ring while I left to go to the bathroom struck me as extremely funny.

When I finally pulled myself together, Brady feigned concern. "You gonna be okay?"

"I'm more than okay, Brady. I'm out of this world."

44

I WOKE UP THE NEXT MORNING AND COULD HEAR BRADY puttering around in the kitchen. Saying, "Coffee, coffee," I shuffled up to him and kissed him on the cheek.

He returned the kiss and handed me a steaming mug. "It's a really nice morning. Let's go out to the porch and drink our coffee."

As we sat outside quietly sipping our morning wake-up brews, Brady joked, "I hope you haven't changed your mind overnight."

"Actually," I said, "there is something I wanted to talk with you about."

He quickly turned toward me. "What's wrong?"

I wet my lips. "My last name. I want to keep it."

He tipped his head. "It's too early in the morning, Mara. Of course you'll keep your last name."

I kissed him on the cheek. "Sorry, just teasing you."

As we flew into the Baja airport, I was stunned by the contrast between the coasts and the desert between them. A twenty-minute walk could take you from cool ocean waters to bone-dry desert cactus country. Never before had I seen an ecological transition as abrupt.

Brady's "nice but not fancy" hotel was absolutely charming. We had a cozy cabana cottage with a view of the ocean to ourselves. Sitting on the cottage porch before dinner, we clinked glasses and sipped the champagne Brady had discovered in the refrigerator.

I swirled my glass and said, "I don't suppose this counts as a honeymoon if we're not husband and wife yet."

He smirked. "I don't think so, Mara. Um, since you brought it up, how and where do you want to get married?"

"In Maine, but other than that, I don't know. Nothing big or fancy, that's for sure. I'd want people closest to me like Angelo, Connor, and Harvey to be there. How about you? Want to invite your parents?"

"No. They loved meeting you but aren't wedding types, if you know what I mean."

"So just a simple ceremony in Angelo's yard with Connor and Harvey?"

Brady finished his champagne and stood. "Simple ceremony, yes." He patted his stomach. "I made dinner reservations in the hotel restaurant, which is supposed to be excellent. I'm starving, so let's *vamonos*."

Over chiles rellenos and enchiladas verdes, we talked about our plan for the next day.

"Neither of us would enjoy a bumpy, hot jeep trip over dirt roads," Brady said, "but we could drive a jeep through wet sand along the beach and see some of the landscape that way."

I nodded. "That sounds good. I've never driven a jeep before, and jumping into the ocean to cool off sounds like an excellent idea."

The jeep was more fun than I could've imagined. Our rental was red, lacked doors, and had oversized tires that splashed water all over the place. The beach we were allowed to drive on was little more than a mile long, so we took our time and stopped often to walk up a bank and check out strange vegetation, including a thirty-foot-high Mexican giant cactus and several tall boojum trees with branches sticking out at right angles and tiny leaves.

"Good lord," I said. "Those boojums look like drawings in a Dr. Seuss children's book."

When we stopped for lunch I splashed around in the water to cool off.

"How many times is that?" Brady teased.

I shrugged. "Maybe ten? You sure were right. A dirt-road jeep trip would've melted me."

Over another traditional Mexican meal that evening—tostadas with refried beans, ground beef, lettuce, tomatoes, and handmade tortillas—Brady explained the next day's logistics.

"You'd better pack tonight, because we'll leave right after breakfast to catch the San Diego plane. Our Boston flight leaves two hours after we land in San Diego, which is plenty of time."

"Oh boy," I teased. "We get to hang out in the first class lounge again."

Despite my teasing, I was amazed how quickly I "adjusted" to the benefits associated with first class. In addition to enjoying the lounge, we didn't have to wait in long lines, had larger seats compared to coach, and could actually lay flat in our seats and sleep. As a result, when we landed in Boston I wasn't a walking zombie.

At six p.m. in Boston, fifty degrees wasn't especially cold in November unless you'd just come from topical weather. Dragging our suitcases, we stepped outside the terminal to wait for the Maine bus.

Wide-eyed, Brady said, "Damn, it's cold!"

Squatting next to my suitcase, I said, "The bus won't be here for twenty minutes. Why don't you pull out a sweater or something? That's what I'm doing."

As usual, a bus marked PORTLAND pulled up to the curb right on time. The driver collected our bags and called out "Portland, Maine" several times as we climbed the stairs into the toasty coach. Less than two hours later we walked through the Portland bus terminal, crossed a street, and found my car. I was very grateful when Brady offered to drive because I didn't wake up until he shook my shoulder and announced that we were home.

45

AFTER A TRIP, I LOVE WAKING UP IN MY OWN BED. ROLLING over, I take in the view from my window—ocean waves running to shore, seagulls diving for fish, a sailboat in the distance.

But this particular morning was different in a wonderfully important way. Brady, to whom I was *engaged*, lay sleeping next to me.

Perhaps sensing that I was awake, Brady stirred and blinked his eyes open. "Morning, beautiful."

"What can I do for my husband-to-be on what looks like a lovely day?"

Sitting up, he said, "Let's see. I'd like scrambled eggs, bacon, raisin bread toasted, cantaloupe, and coffee with cream."

"There's coffee and a couple of eggs in the fridge, I think."

"Why don't you go ahead a take a shower, Mara? Let's see what I can drum up in the kitchen."

Rubbing my wet hair with a towel, I walked downstairs forty-five minutes later to witness a minor miracle. A platter on the kitchen table held French toast smothered in melting butter, and next to it a compote of blueberries, strawberries, and blackberries.

I draped the towel over a chair. "Good lord, Brady. How did you manage all this?"

He shrugged. "Everything was in the freezer, and the rest was simply creative genius. Coffee is on the counter with some mugs. Go help yourself."

I drank the last of my coffee and finished a second helping of French toast. "Excellent breakfast, Brady. I guess you can stay."

Standing, he said, "And you are doing the dishes, right?"

"Sure thing. The dishes go in the dishwasher, right?"

"You know," I said as we rode into town, "I'm not used to going back to work after a vacation. It feels weird."

"As opposed to a research cruise," he said.

I nodded. "Right. After a research trip there are samples to sort, data to compile, and equipment to check. Today, I'll walk into my office and hardly remember what I was doing before I left."

"No worries, Mara," he said. "In an hour or two, shark cages, Baja, and all the rest will seem like a distant dream."

Brady was right. By noon when my "to do" pile had shrunk by half, I stared at a photo of the *Guadalupe Explorer* as a reminder of what we'd done and seen.

The photo was still on my computer's desktop when Harvey walked in. Standing next to my chair, she said, "That's an unusual-looking ship. What are those big cage things on the deck?"

"Shark cages. You go down in them and watch sharks."

"Better you than me, Mara. It looks absolutely terrifying. Can you and Brady come over for dinner tonight and show us your photos?"

"We can," I said, "and we have some exciting news to share." I wiggled my left ring finger.

She reached for my hand. "Oh, Mara, it's absolutely gorgeous. I'm so happy for both of you!"

"It's a family ring. Brady's mom gave it to him when we all had dinner in Santa Cruz."

"Any idea when you'll get married?"

"Sometime soon. Angelo's back yard would be perfect, so we are thinking of doing it there, but I haven't even told him."

"He'll be delighted, Mara. You know that. And Connor is ordained, so he can marry you."

That evening, Brady and I clinked glasses with Harvey and Connor and enjoyed a celebratory bottle of champagne before dinner. "But, Connor," I said, "mum's the word, since Angelo doesn't know yet."

Brady projected his computer presentation of the shark cruise onto Connor's big-screen television. Viewing photos of the *Guadalupe Explorer* on a TV made the trip seem unreal, not anything I'd actually experienced. Had I really been enclosed in a cage underwater with sharks swimming tens of feet away and sometimes even closer? And had a piece of bologna actually drifted to our cage and announced its olfactory presence before the ship's crew managed to haul us up out of the water?

Brady's detailed account of the great whites, including their behavior, threatened status, and global distribution, shifted the focus away from the danger of shark diving until Harvey brought it up again.

"Brady, everything has its pros and cons, of course. I'd like to know how dangerous shark cage diving is for people and for the sharks."

Nodding, Brady said, "It's a very good question. If people follow rules like keeping hands and feet inside the cage and not attracting sharks with bait, I'd say it's very safe. Of course you've got to go with people who know what they are doing—the divemaster in the cage with you, crew, and captain of the ship. And it's critical that all those people care about the welfare of the sharks, not just of the paying customers. Sharks are critically endangered worldwide, and I hope that cage diving and other shark tourism activities help people understand that."

46

DELIGHTED BY OUR ANNOUNCEMENT, ANGELO SHOOK Brady's hand and embraced me.

"Oh, *mio dio*," he said, "Mara and Brady, this is glorious news."

I kissed him on the cheek. "Connor will do the honors, and we'd love to have the ceremony in your yard very soon before it gets too cold."

He beamed. "Of course, Mara, of course. And we'll celebrate with a real Italian wedding menu, I assume?"

"Angelo, that would be lovely. But not too much food, please, since it's just us. Would you like Angelica to come?"

He nodded. "Oh, yes. With Angelica there, the day will be even more special for me."

We set the wedding day three days later on a Saturday when the weatherman forecast seasonable warmth and sun. That done, I faced a much more difficult decision—what in heaven's name was I going to wear?

Harvey is the only person I'd ever known with a walk-in closet, never mind one organized by season. Less than a week before my wedding, I was nothing but grateful for her ample, diverse attire. Grateful too that we were the same size.

Standing in the closet, she asked, "I assume you want something comfortable and tasteful but not too bride-y."

I nodded. "Right, definitely not too bride-y."

She held up a tan pantsuit. "Too un-bride-y?"

I nodded. "Yeah. That says business meeting, not getting married."

"There's a white dress in here somewhere I wore five or six years ago. Ah, here it is." She pulled out a long, fitted, cream-colored dress made of lace.

I held the lacy arm my hand. "It's truly lovely, Harvey, but it's a lot more you than me. I'm afraid I wouldn't feel comfortable wearing that."

Looking at the dress, she tipped her head. "Hmm. I see what you mean."

Harvey reached into the back of the closet and came out with a more down-to-earth knee-length white dress with a V-shaped neckline.

I wiggled out of my jeans, pulled off my T-shirt, and slipped the dress over my head. "Harvey, zip this up, would you?"

She walked behind me, pulled up the zipper, turned me around, and grinned. "Well, Mara, I think you've found your dress. Go look in the mirror."

I stood in front of her door-length mirror and ran my hands down the smooth, silky fabric. The dress fit me perfectly.

"What is Brady wearing?" Harvey asked.

"He said something about black slacks and a white shirt."

"I'll bet he's never seen you in a dress like that," she said.

"You got that right. I'm not sure he's seen me in any dress."

She tipped her head. "Are you going anywhere right after the wedding?"

I shrugged. "We've just come back from a pretty amazing trip, so probably not."

"Well," she said, "after Brady spends all day looking at you in that dress, you might want to make some special plans ahead of time."

Later, as we nibbled almond cookies and sipped tea in Harvey's kitchen, I thanked Harvey. "Like always, you've been a huge help. It means a lot to me."

She laughed. "Are you kidding? This is a blast. You, my best girlfriend, finally found your soul mate, and I can help with a wedding dress."

"Plus Connor will marry us. How great is that?"

"Do you think Dr. Dixon should know about the wedding?" she asked. "It certainly would be the courteous thing to do."

"Good lord, Harvey, you are absolutely right. Brady and I should make an appointment with Dixon right away." I grinned. "See? This is why you are department chair and I'm not!"

That evening, Brady and I enjoyed some before-dinner wine in the living room. It was too cold to sit outside on the deck, so I'd asked him to get a fire going in the fireplace so we could enjoy it from the couch.

"What is it about a crackling sound that's so cozy?" I asked.

Pulling me closer, he kissed the top of my head. "I don't know. Chestnuts roasting on an open fire and all that?"

"You did a good job with it, by the way."

"Your wood was really dry, which made all the difference. What kind of hardwood is it?"

"Maple and oak," I said. "There's no pitch, and they burn well. Did you know that Maine is something like ninety percent forested? That's the highest percentage of any state."

"Huh," he said. "What kinds of trees, and who owns it?"

"Let's see. Red and sugar maple, oaks, birch, pine, spruce, balsam fir. And about ninety-five percent is privately owned. Like a lot of New England, much of Maine was cleared for farms in the seventeen and eighteen hundreds. When people discovered all that rich, deep soil in the Midwest, Maine's farms were abandoned. That's why you see all those stone walls snaking through our forests."

"Changing the subject," he said, "you were in a pretty good mood after visiting with Harvey today. Anything in particular?"

"She's got this big walk-in closet full of clothes, including what's going to be my dress."

"Which I won't see until our wedding day, I assume?"

"It's white, that's all I can say."

47

I WAS ABLE TO MAKE AN APPOINTMENT WITH DR. DIXON the next morning at ten.

"May I tell him what the appointment is about?"

"It's a personal matter and nothing serious," I said.

Dixon looked concerned as he invited Brady and me to sit down and tell him what this was all about.

"Well, sir," I said, "Brady and I intend to marry next week. We wanted to let you know."

He clapped his hands. "Well, congratulations, both of you. Mara, I must admit I've been worried you might leave us for Scripps."

"As you know," I said, "MOI is in my blood, so to speak. It'd be very difficult for me to leave."

Dixon nodded. "Yes, yes. And I suppose you'd like us to offer Brady a permanent position?"

"Well, that's not why...that is..." I stammered.

Dixon smiled. "Mara, I realize that's not why you are here. Actually, I've been thinking that a well-known shark biologist would be an excellent addition to MOI's team. The publicity alone would benefit us, never mind Brady's grant support."

Brady leaned forward in his chair. "Sir, am I to understand that you might offer me a permanent position here?"

"Yes, that's right." Grinning, Dixon said, "Of course, I need to pass this by our department chair, but I suspect that Harvey will have no objection."

After dinner, Brady and I stood outside on the porch to watch the sunset.

Touching my arm, Brady said, "You've been kind of quiet all evening, Mara. Are you okay?"

I shrugged. "Really? Guess I'm getting nervous."

Brady knit his brow. "About marrying me?"

I turned toward him. "No, no. Of course not."

"Well, what then?"

"Everything is going too smoothly. I'm worried something's going to happen."

Brady grinned. "Take it easy, Mara. Everything will be fine."

The next morning, my cell phone announced an incoming call. I pushed myself up to a sitting position and glanced at the time. Who could be calling me at six a.m.?"

It was Harvey. "Sorry to call so early, but you might want to turn on the weather station."

"Why? What's happening?"

"I'll leave that to the weather guys. Ring me later."

I stumbled downstairs, got the coffee going, padded into the living room, switched on the television, and selected the weather station.

In my groggy state it was hard to take in, but I got the gist. A Caribbean hurricane, name of Leonine, was barreling up the east coast headed for New England.

"Folks," the weather lady said, "Leonine the lioness is sure living up to her namesake. This is an extremely fast-moving storm that should slam into Cape Cod the day after tomorrow and then continue up the coast. A landmass small as the Cape won't moderate this storm at all, so at this point we're calling this a category three hurricane for the entire New England area. That's a major hurricane with winds up to one hundred fifty miles an hour. Location of the highest winds depends on the exact path the storm takes, and we will give you an update on that as soon as we can."

Even without my morning coffee I understood what was about to happen. In forty-eight hours, on our wedding day, a category three hurricane was going to slam into the Maine coast.

Wearing jeans, no shirt or shoes, and rubbing his eyes, Brady shuffled into the kitchen fifteen minutes later. Seated at the kitchen table, I stared at my half-empty mug of coffee.

"Jesus, Mara. What's happened? Has someone died?"

Blinking, I looked at him. "Died? No, no. A cat three hurricane will get here on our wedding day."

"Blimey," he said. "That's unexpected, and it's the second time a big storm has messed up our plans."

"Brady, I'm *so* upset. We can't get married in a hurricane."

"Give me a moment. I need some coffee."

He sipped the coffee and put down the mug. "We'll just have to move it up."

"Move what?" I asked.

"The wedding. If everyone can make it, which I'm guessing they will, let's get married this afternoon. It looks pretty nice outside now."

I stared at him for a moment and said, "Brady, that's brilliant."

He kissed my hand. "Dear, you can call me brilliant anytime."

I first called Angelo, who, not surprisingly, had already anticipated the problem. "An outside wedding in a hurricane would be *antipatico*, my dear. Most unpleasant. Yes, this afternoon would be very much better."

"What about the food?" I asked

"It's a very small group, Mara. No difficulty there."

48

"I TAKE YOU, BRADY, TO BE MY HUSBAND, TO HAVE AND TO hold from this day forward, for better or worse, for richer or poorer, in sickness and in health, to love and to cherish, until we are parted by death. This is my solemn *vow.*"

"And I take you, Mara, to be my wife, to have and to hold from this day forward, for better or worse, for richer or poorer, in sickness and in health, to love and to cherish, until we are parted by death. This is my solemn *vow.*"

"Mara, Brady," Connor said, "you are now wed. Brady, you may kiss your bride."

Brady pulled me close, kissed me gently, stepped back, and grinned. Behind us, Angelo, Angelica, and Harvey clapped their hands and laughed.

"*Eccellente*," Angelo called out. "Please come inside for champagne and an Italian wedding meal!"

Brady and I held hands as we followed the others toward the house. Leaning close, he whispered in my ear, "You look amazing in that dress."

I hardly recognized the dining room as we walked in. A long table draped in white damask was set with sparkling crystal glasses and silver plus platters of classic Italian food—mini meatballs simmered in tomato sauce, tomato bruschetta, ravioli, and chicken marsala—within reach of each place setting.

"Mara and Brady," Angelo said, "the two chairs at the head of the table are yours. Everyone else, please find a seat and help yourselves to champagne so that we can toast this lovely couple!"

Laughing, I managed to drink some bubbly and hand my glass to Brady without spilling it all over his lap. Brady held up the champagne and invited everyone to enjoy the remarkable feast.

As the sounds of laugher and chitchat rose, I scanned the room. All the people I loved and cared deeply about were right here to help Brady and me celebrate our special day. The realization brought tears to my eyes.

Leaning closer, Brady murmured, "Are you all right?"

I kissed his cheek. "More all right than I've been in a long, long time."

When it looked like everyone had eaten their fill, Angelo stood to say a few words.

He said, "Two extraordinary people, Bridget and Carlos Tusconi, cannot be with us today, although I have no doubt they are enjoying this celebration from a very special place. Since most of you never met the Tusconis, I'd like to tell you a little about them."

The room went quiet.

"A woman with strong convictions, smart, and loyal as the day is long, Bridget lived up to her Irish heritage. She was also a real beauty, a trait she obviously passed along to her daughter. An Italian, Carlos was generous, funny, intelligent, and a man for whom family was everything. He and Bridget were absolutely delighted when Mara was born, and I was honored to call her my goddaughter." He looked in our direction. "And Brady, they would certainly have loved to call you son."

Angelo held up his glass. "To Bridget and Carlos Tusconi."

I stood and repeated, "To Bridget and Carlos Tusconi," with everyone else as tears rolled down my cheeks.

"All right, everyone," Angelo said. "There's lots more bubbly to enjoy, plus tiramisu."

After Brady and I sat down again to enjoy dessert, he leaned closer. "I've never had tiramisu. What's in it?"

"Are you serious?" I asked.

"Mara, wife, just tell me what it is."

"Let's see. Tiramisu is a coffee-flavored Italian dessert. You dip ladyfingers in coffee and make layers with a whipped mixture of eggs and sugar, plus mascarpone cheese flavored with cocoa."

"Huh," he said, "So does the word *tiramisu* mean anything?"

I shrugged. "Honestly, I never wondered about that. Let's ask Angelo."

Angelo, of course, knew the answer. "It's Italian for 'pick me up' or 'cheer me up,' and some Italians believe the dessert is strong aphrodisiac."

As Brady burst out laughing, I said, "You've got to be kidding."

49

AFTER THE PARTY, I GAVE BRADY THE CAR KEYS AND ASKED him to drive us home.

He frowned. "Anything wrong?"

"Not a bit," I said. "I'm tired, happy, and maybe a little bit tipsy, that's all."

After we climbed the stairs up the porch Brady said, "Wait right here for a second."

He pushed the kitchen door open, walked back, swept me off my feet, and said, "This is what the groom does, right?"

I kissed him on the cheek. "It is, husband of mine. Just be super careful of the dress when you put me down."

Inside the kitchen I said, "Be right back," went upstairs to change into jeans and a T-shirt, and found Brady fixed on the living room television a few minutes later. He had tuned in the Weather Channel and looked worried.

"Anything wrong?"

"There's another intense hurricane barreling toward us. The weather guys seem really concerned."

I shrugged. "Another storm? You know they exaggerate."

He shook his head. "Sit down and listen. This sounds pretty bad."

The weather guy was speaking. "We have a *second* potential category three hurricane heading our way. No doubt about it, this could be a very dangerous storm, and we are taking every precaution to be prepared and ensure everyone's safety. Mainers with small boats should absolutely get them ashore. Also, make sure your backup generators are working and that you have fuel for them.

"Hurricane category three or higher storms are rare in New England because cooler sea temperatures and prevailing winds usually weaken storms or bend them eastward. But because Long Island and New England jut out into the western Atlantic, they are vulnerable to very fast-moving tropical storms moving north, and cat three storms do hit this area every 90-100 years.

"Since very few of you were alive in 1938, we would like you to briefly review the damage caused by the '38 hurricane. An estimated seven hundred people died, and over fifty-five thousand homes were destroyed or damaged, with property losses around five billion dollars. Folks, here's the bottom line. Do not underestimate the damage this storm could cause. Be prepared and start that preparation right now."

"Good lord, Brady, I had no idea this storm was so bad. Before it gets dark, let's go outside and bring anything that could blow away into the garage."

Forty-five minutes later, we'd carried the kayaks and paddles, porch furniture, umbrella, and grill into the garage, leaving just enough room for my Subaru. With Brady's help, I inched the car into the garage and secured the door.

"I know you've got a generator," Brady said, "but what about gasoline to operate it?"

"No worries," I said. "When the power goes out here, we've got no lights, heat, stove, plus no running water. I've lived through that too many times, and believe me, it's no fun. So yes, the generator works, and we've got plenty of propane. If there's a power outage, the generator automatically clicks on."

Protected from spitting rain by our foul-weather gear, Brady and I stood on the porch and watched the rapidly approaching storm. Within a matter of minutes, gusty winds became a howling tempest, and we had to shout to be heard.

"Sorry, Brady," I yelled. "Didn't catch that."

He leaned closer. "Already the ocean's become a churning maelstrom. It's stunning!"

Stinging rain pelted my cheeks, and I held up my hands to cover my face. "This isn't fun anymore. I'm going inside."

In the kitchen we stepped out of our dripping raingear. I quickly wiped my face and handed Brady the towel.

"How about I get a fire going in the fireplace," I said, "while you hang up this wet stuff in the bathroom shower?"

Once more we enjoyed the crackling fire from the couch.

"Got a question for you," Brady said. "Why does wood crackle in a fire?"

I shrugged. "That's one of those things I've never thought to ask. Any ideas?"

"That popping noise sounds like gas expanding. Does that make sense?"

"Yes, but I'm guessing that water trapped in the wood is also released when the wood burns. Firewood is never completely dry, of course."

Outside, the storm was making itself heard.

"Sometimes during a bad storm like this I wonder if there's a boat with fishermen on it out there somewhere smashing up and down in the waves," I said. "People don't realize that making a living on the ocean fishing, lobstering, or whatever is extremely dangerous work."

"What's the main hazard for lobstermen?" Brady asked.

"It's horrible to even imagine, but sometimes their legs or arms get tangled in a trap line and they are pulled overboard and drown."

Brady shook his head. "Good god. How absolutely dreadful."

50

"**B**RADY, ON A MORE POSITIVE NOTE," I SAID, "ARE YOU AT all hungry?"

He shrugged. "Given all we've eaten today I shouldn't be, but I am. What do we have?"

"Not much, but I could make us omelets."

"Can't remember the last time I had an omelet, but that does sound good."

I'd just gotten the makings of an omelet out of the fridge— eggs, cheese, onion, mushrooms, and cream—when the lights flickered for a moment and then went out.

Still in the living room, Brady called out, "You okay? Should I look for flashlights?"

"No, the backup generator will come on in less than a minute."

Standing in the dark, I waited for what seemed a whole lot longer than a minute. Finally, the generator growled and the lights flicked on again.

"See?" I said. "Works like a charm."

"Does everyone out this way have a generator?" Brady asked.

"Tall trees with leaves and elevated electric wires are a bad combination in a big storm, and they are everywhere in the state. Without a generator we could be without power for a week or more. Living by candlelight sounds romantic, but it gets old real fast. Cooking on a camp stove plus carrying in water for drinking and everything else does too."

The next morning, a diminished version of the storm was still with us. It was raining, but lightly, and feeling housebound

I pulled on my rain gear and walked outside to check out the damage. Leaves and tree branches were haphazardly strewn everywhere, and the beach in front of my house was littered with seaweed, pieces of marine rope, and lots of unidentifiable plastic debris.

I walked back into the kitchen to describe what I'd seen. "We've got some cleanup to do, but it's really not too bad."

Seated at the kitchen table, Brady stared at his computer and shook his head. "Glad to hear it, but I wish things were as good at MOI."

"Why? What's happened?"

"Looks like some pretty serious damage. The dock really took a beating. Apparently, it's half gone."

"Oh, my god. What about the research vessels?"

"Two were in Spruce Harbor, but they rode out the storm offshore and are okay."

"And the lab buildings?"

He shrugged. "There's nothing here about that. We'll have to drive into town to find out, but the basement of the biology building has got to be flooded."

I fell into the chair across from him. "This can't be happening again."

"The building flooded before?"

I nodded. "Yup. A huge, sudden spring rainstorm, and I found it. When I got there, the basement's bottom step was already underwater. Walkways between the tables down there were swirling streams."

He gasped. "What about all the saltwater aquaria?"

"They were up on tables, but inches from being swamped with rainwater. All those marine animals—fish, crabs, starfish, squid, mussels, clams—were about to die in brackish water. It was absolutely horrible."

"So what did you do?"

"Called 911 and set out to rescue Homer."

"Don't tell me you walked through that maelstrom to save a lobster."

"Maybe you don't understand, but I *had* to. If freshwater flooded his tank he would've died. After I made the call, I pushed my way through the water, lifted him out of his tank into a bucket with some salt water, and carried him back to the stairs."

"But you said it was spring. That water must've been absolutely freezing cold!"

I nodded. "It sure was. When the first responders found me, I was hypothermic. The rest is pretty much a blur, but I ended up in the hospital."

He tipped his head and studied me. "That's an amazing story, Mara. You were very brave."

I reached for his hand. "Thanks for not calling me stupid."

He kissed my fingers. "You are very, very far from stupid."

Back outside, we loaded four buckets with litter from the beach and piled strewn branches in one corner of the yard.

Frowning, Brady peered into the woods between the yard and main road.

"There's some pretty large trees blocking the dirt road. I don't suppose you have a chainsaw?"

I shook my head. "Nope, just a couple of hand saws for cutting wood."

Two hours later, we cleared the access road of branches and small trees and stood beside the paved road into Spruce Harbor.

I rolled my shoulders. "That gives you respect for the guys who do that type of work every day."

"You've got that right," Brady said. "That's real work. In comparison, what we do is play."

51

THE RIDE INTO SPRUCE HARBOR TOOK TWICE AS LONG AS usual. The road was littered with debris, so we had to dodge tree limbs and crunch branches strewn everywhere. Halfway there, we waited for fifteen minutes as police used chainsaws to remove a good-sized tree from the middle of the road and direct traffic around the remains afterward.

I parked in MOI's lot behind the biology building, climbed out of the car, and gasped at an unthinkable sight. About three quarters of the two-hundred-foot-long dock was gone, a ragged remnant jutting out into the sea the only proof of its existence.

"Absolutely astonishing," Brady said. "At least the research ships rode the storm out at sea, so they are all right."

I shook my head. "This can't be happening. That dock was where you waved at friends, your family, and other scientists as their ship pulled away for a research cruise and where you waited for them when they came back. When I was a kid, Angelo would bring me to the dock so I could catch a glimpse of my parents as their ship pulled into Spruce Harbor. It's just, I don't know…"

A voice behind us finished my thought. "It's a goddamn shame, that's what it is."

Together, Brady and I turned around as Betty Butz walked closer. A fixture in Spruce Harbor, Betty was a bullet of a woman who swore like a sailor and wore a plaid flannel shirt and leather boots, even in summer.

"But I saw a whole lot worse down in Woods Hole with Hurricane Gloria," Betty said. "Oceanographic dock ripped in half, boats smashed against the rocks, glass all over—it was like a bomb hit us. Sailboats got stranded way up on rocks, lawns, you name it. It took helicopters to lift some of them up into the sky and back down into the water, if you can believe that."

She eyed Brady up and down, glanced at me, and grinned. "I'd say you two are, what do they call it, a unit? Yeah, that's it. A unit."

Brady extended his hand. "Brady MacFarlane, Dr. Butz. It's a real pleasure to meet you."

She gave Brady's hand three quick shakes. "Call me Betty. And you are the shark guy, right?"

Betty winked at me. "Gotta say, he's a good lookin' man, Mara, not like that Ted character. Always thought he lacked character, zip, spunk. What happened to that Ted, anyway? Haven't seen him around."

"He's down in Woods Hole," I said, "and he's taken up with a graduate student."

Betty slapped her thigh. "See? That's just what I mean. A grad student, the dumbass."

Before I could respond she said, "Well, I gotta go. Now, Brady, you take good care of this lady or you'll hear from me."

And with that, Betty turned around and limped toward the parking lot.

When she was out of earshot, Brady said, "Remarkable woman."

"I'm surprised you know anything about Betty," I said.

He grinned. "In Woods Hole, folks see Betty as either a women's lib idol or a total pain in the butt and not much in between. In the fifties she was irate that she couldn't be the only woman on a research cruise. She needed to have a secretary, lion tamer, whatever, as a companion, so long as that person was female."

"Because…?"

"If Betty got sick on a trip," he said, "there had to be a female on board to take care of her."

"Oh, I see."

"Betty threatened to come aboard as a visiting male and let the medics find out what she really was if it came to that."

"Whoa, I wouldn't want to be that medic for anything," I said.

Brady and I had only walked a hundred feet back to the parking lot when it happened. A woman screamed, "Stop, Charlie, stop!" and then she, Brady, and I watched horror-struck as a child ran from her side and headed for the shattered dock. Seemingly frozen with fear, she reached out as if to grab him but didn't move.

Without a thought, I turned around sprinted after the little boy.

For a little kid, Charlie was a very good runner. He reached the pier well before I did and kept on going. I'd just set foot on the dock when he jumped off the end and disappeared.

52

I THREW OFF MY RAINCOAT AND SHIRT AS I SPRINTED DOWN the dock, pulled off my jeans at the ragged edge, and jumped in.

The frigid ocean was so shocking I screamed and came up gagging. Treading water, I hacked up seawater and spun around in circles. The little boy wasn't anywhere on the surface, so my addled brain told me he must've gone under.

I took a breath, dove down, and scanned the bottom for little Charlie. Visibility was good, thank goodness, but seawater stung my eyes and I had to keep blinking to see anything at all. I was just about to give up when I spotted him lying on the bottom next to the end piling. Above water again, I coughed up more seawater, sucked in a good breath, and dove down.

Charlie didn't move when I reached out to touch him. Praying he wasn't dead, I grabbed his shirt and pushed hard off the bottom. When we both surfaced, two hands reached down from the dock, grasped the boy under his armpits, and pulled him up to safety.

Panting from exertion and excitement, I doggy-paddled toward shore and stumbled through shallow water up to the sand.

Brady wrapped my shoulders in a beach towel he'd gotten somewhere and pulled me close. "Mara, you brave idiot, are you okay?"

In between coughs I managed to communicate that, yes, I was just fine.

Brady said, "The kid, who seems none the worse for wear, is farther up the beach with his mother and a couple of guys from MOI. I assume they've called some medics to check him out."

After a couple more coughs I asked, "Was that you who pulled him up at the end of the dock?"

"Yeah, that was me," Brady said. "If you hadn't surfaced with the kid, I would've jumped in to get both of you."

I'd stopped coughing by the time the boy's mother walked over. Tears in her eyes, she took my hand. "You saved my Carlos. There's no way in the world I can thank you enough."

I tipped my head. "Carlos?"

"Yes, dear. That's his birth name, but we call him Charlie."

I looked over at the boy. "Well, that's an amazing coincidence. My father was called Carlos, and I've never met anyone else with the same name."

The shivering started as I watched Charlie's mom walk back to be with her son. "Shower," I said. "H-hot shower."

Rubbing my arms, Brady asked, "Where's the closest one?"

"B-basement."

"Basement it is," Brady said. "I picked up the clothes you threw on the dock."

I stepped out of the shower a couple of hundred gallons of near-boiling water later, toweled off, and dressed. Events of the last couple of hours were already a blur. Had we really cleared my access road, skirted downed trees as we rode into town, and chatted with Betty Butz about Hurricane Gloria before Charlie raced down the pier and jumped off?

Leaning against the basement wall, Brady greeted me as I emerged from the women's shower room. "You are a new person, right?"

"Sure am," I said. "It's a surprise you even recognize me."

"You must be exhausted," he said. "Want to head home?"

I shook my head. "Let's finish what we came here to do and see what's happening with Harvey."

We climbed the basement steps and walked into a lobby humming with activity. Scientists, technicians, and grad students ran up and down stairs, called out to each other, and yanked open doors to their floors.

"Good lord," I said. "The elevators aren't working, of course. People are desperate to find out what's happened to their walk-in incubators and everything else."

Brady shrugged. "Walk-in incubators?"

"Oh, you know," I said, "people use them for everything from growing seaweed in big vats to cultivating oyster spat before their trip out to the oyster beds."

"What about sensitive devices like mass spectrometers?" Brady asked.

"That's why I want to check on Harvey. She calls her mass spec the instrument that loves to tease her. One day it works fine, and the next she can't get a decent measurement come hell or high water. I can't imagine what a major electrical outage has done to it."

We walked into Harvey's second floor lab, where she was clearly preoccupied with the pesky instrument in her glassed-in "cell." As we waited, I noticed *Marine Chemists' Analytical Methods* on one of the lab tables, picked the book up, and handed it to Brady.

"The first time I met Cary she told me this was the marine chemists' bible. She wanted to be an oceanographer since she was a little girl." Tearing up, I shook my head. "Oh, Brady. So much has happened since then. I just can't take it all in."

Brady pulled me close and stroked my hair. "Mara, things will get better. They just will."

I wanted to believe him. I really did.

53

HARVEY STEPPED OUT OF THE INSTRUMENT ROOM, AND the door closed behind her with a whoosh.

"Everything okay in there?" I asked.

"For a change, that vexatious machine is behaving itself."

"Vexatious?"

"You know," she said, "annoying, exasperating, irksome."

"Mischievous?" I added.

"That too. But you didn't stop by to practice the dictionary, so what's up?"

"Let's see," Brady said. "Mara saved a little boy named Charlie about an hour ago."

"Whoa," Harvey said. "Saved how?"

I shrugged. "Before his mother could stop him, Charlie bolted down the MOI pier and leaped off the end. So I ran after him and jumped down into the water to get him."

Harvey frowned. "Down as in under the water?"

"The kid sank like a stone. I found him on the bottom and pulled him up."

"I take it both you and Charlie are okay," she said.

I shrugged. "Yeah."

Brady pulled me closer. "Actually, Mara was amazing, and as you can imagine Charlie's mother thinks Mara's superwoman."

"Connor is gonna love this story," Harvey said. "So why don't you two come over for dinner tonight and go through the whole episode from start to finish?"

"Great," Brady and I said in unison.

"Brady, just one last thing before I get back to the beast," Harvey said.

Brady raised an eyebrow.

"This superwoman stuff is going to happen from time to time, so you'll need to get used to it."

As I drove to Harvey and Connor's house that evening, Brady said, "Before we get there, you've got to tell me what Harvey meant by my getting used to the, um, superwoman stuff."

I tried to laugh, but it came out as a cough. Recovering, I said, "Oh, you know Harvey. She's just exaggerating."

Brady didn't answer, but I suspect he didn't believe me.

As usual, Harvey, Brady, and I chatted in the living room before dinner, and Connor added his two cents now and then from the kitchen. As I expected, the main topic of discussion was the storm, and my efforts to direct the focus away from that meteorological event ultimately failed.

Wiping his hands on a dishtowel, Connor walked into the living room and asked, "What's this I hear about Mara saving the day?"

Starting with, "Connor, you should've been there," Brady gave a blow-by-blow of the whole episode. Then, of course, he wanted to hear Harvey's explanation of the superwoman moniker.

Alternating as narrator, Harvey and Connor described a half dozen of my "exploits," as they called them, over the last few years.

"In British Columbia, Mara was forced to jump overboard into the freezing cold ocean and nearly died, but she was saved from drowning in a kelp bed by a seal."

"Mara found a lobsterman's body under his aquaculture raft and eventually solved the murder."

"She went down in a submersible to see the Hanging Gardens—that's Maine's deepwater reef."

"A while back, Mara spoke to an auditorium full of reporters and explained why scientists say they 'have confidence' in their data versus 'believing' their data."

"She confronted international eel traffickers and saved Harvey's life."

I held up my hand. "Enough, already. Could we *please* change the subject and talk about something besides me?"

54

BRADY DROVE HOME, AND ON THE WAY HE ASKED THE question I knew was coming.

"Ya know all those so-called exploits Connor and Harvey told us about?"

"Exploits?" I punted.

"They were exaggerating, right?"

"Um, well, ah…"

"So all that happened? You were saved by a seal, found a lobsterman's body under his raft, and everything else?"

I shrugged. "I had help with the eel traffickers."

He snorted. "I'll bet there's more they didn't bother to mention."

"What can I say, Brady? Sometimes trouble seems to follow me around. It's one of the reasons why Ted…why he…"

Brady pulled the car to the side of the road and turned to face me. "Hey, if it sounded like I was criticizing you, I'm sorry, because that wasn't the case. Maybe someday you can entertain me with some of your escapades, but only if you want to. Mara, you love adventures. I know that. It's one of the reasons I'm crazy about you, because I love adventures as well. And now we can share them together."

Sniffing, I blinked back tears. "I'm so very glad, thank you. And, um, do you have a tissue?"

Back home I carried a mug of herbal tea with honey into the living room and joined Brady on the couch. Holding up the mug, I said, "Sure you don't want any?"

He shrugged. "Thanks, no, but I've been thinking about something Harvey said and would really appreciate your input."

Sipping the tea, I settled back on the couch to listen.

"Harvey mentioned that you spoke to an auditorium full of reporters about the nature of science. When was that?"

I shrugged. "A couple of years ago. It bugs me, you know, that people say things like scientists *believe* in global warming. Scientists might tell their children that they believe in Santa or the tooth fairy, but as you know you very well, our interest in warming has nothing to do with belief. We work with the data and determine the degree to which it does or does not support our hypotheses. I was trying to help reporters understand that."

"Got it," he said. "And that was here at MOI?"

"Yeah, in the auditorium."

"Okay, here's the idea," he said. "I'd love to give a talk to reporters and people who write for magazines, newspapers, and other popular outlets about all the crazy misconceptions people have about sharks and why those fallacies are so dangerous for an endangered species. I'd want to explain that, in just the last half-century, humans have caused a staggering worldwide drop in the number of sharks that swim the open oceans. I would tell them that over three quarters of oceanic shark species are now threatened with extinction, which jeopardizes marine ecosystems and food security of people worldwide. People care about butterflies, and I want them to care about sharks. But we've got a very, very small window to save them."

"How about adding a historical take?" I said. "There's that painting by John Singleton Copley in the National Gallery of Art."

"*Watson and the Shark* is an attention getter for sure," Brady said. "Bleeding and helpless, a naked boy struggles to stay above water as sailors rescue him from the open jaw of a huge shark.

It's based on an actual event but might be too sensational for this audience."

Nodding, I slid the mug onto the coffee table. "Brady, whatever you decide about the specifics, this is a fabulous idea. I'm sure Harvey and Dixon would love it. The event could be invitation-only for reporters and high-dollar MOI donors. MOI's publicity people could contact reporters from Augusta, Portland, and other New England cities."

"I'm liking this more and more," he said. "We'll have to come up with a really good title for the program."

"I guess something like You Are More Likely to Be Killed by Your Toaster Than a Shark won't do?" I asked.

He snorted. "It's catchy but a little too cute."

The next morning we found Harvey in her official department office. She was on the phone and waved us in as she finished a phone call.

"Anything interesting?" I asked.

"As I've said before, much of this job isn't a bit interesting," she said. "That was a vendor trying to convince me to exclusively order Maine-sourced toilet paper, if you can believe it."

I shrugged. "Actually, I can. Mainers can be awfully distrustful of anything out of state, especially if it is from Massachusetts."

Brady snorted. "You've got to be kidding."

"Well, there's a long history there," Harvey said. "The two states used to be one, but that ended when Massachusetts got rich by selling Maine lumber for a lot more than they paid and not sharing the profit. That Mainers were underrepresented in the Massachusetts legislature didn't help either. The bill for Maine statehood was signed in 1820. But you didn't drop by for a political lesson. What's up?"

55

HARVEY NODDED AS WE EXPLAINED BRADY'S SHARK TALK proposal and clapped her hands when we finished. "It's a terrific idea. Dixon will love it, and the publicity folks will have a field day. Have you thought about a date?"

I shook my head. "We hadn't gotten that far."

She flipped open her computer. "Give me a second while I scan the calendar. Let's see, Earth Day was in April, so that won't work, and Shark Day was months ago."

"Really?" I said. "Shark Day?"

"Look it up," Brady said, "and World Introvert Day is in January, along with Humiliation Day. But you've got to wait until April for No Housework and Save an Elephant Days."

"Sorry to interrupt, but I've got the perfect date," Harvey said. "MOI was officially founded in November ten days from now. That's not much time for the publicity folks, but they'll manage. Have you thought about a title?"

"We have," I said. "But I'm pretty sure you'll think it's too cutesy."

"Give me a try."

Brady cleared his throat. "You Are More Likely to Be Killed by Your Toaster Than a Shark."

Harvey smirked. "Pretentiously artistic is what I'd call that. I'll ask publicity to work on a title and check it out with you."

The next day Harvey assembled what she called the "shark talk committee"—Sandra from publicity along with Brady and me—in the upstairs lounge. Frederick Dixon stopped by for a few minutes, but the fact that MOI's director had taken the time at all said a lot about the importance of Brady's presentation.

Brady turned to Sandra. "Shark conservation covers a lot of territory, so I'd really appreciate your input about what's most important for this audience."

"I can imagine," she said. "Give me an idea of what you usually emphasize when you talk to a group of non-scientists."

Brady nodded. "I usually begin with wild misconceptions people have—like how many people are killed annually by sharks versus the number of sharks people slaughter for shark fin soup. Besides that, the number of unprovoked shark bites worldwide is extremely low, especially given how many folks swim, surf, paddleboard, and all the rest. And even when they know sharks are around, people do the dumbest things."

"Huh," Sandra said. "Like what?"

"In places where there are sharks, signs on beaches warn swimmers not get in the water at night or during twilight hours when sharks are especially active, but they do it anyway. And there are other warnings that people ignore, like not entering the water if they are bleeding—that's because sharks have amazing olfactory receptors—and not wearing shiny jewelry, which attracts sharks."

Sandra nodded. "Really interesting. So where in the U.S. are the most people killed by sharks?"

"Florida, Hawaii, and California. Of course you know about the recent fatality in Maine, but that was extremely unusual."

"Anything you want to say about that?"

Brady shrugged. "I want to respect her privacy, so it's very tricky. Probably not."

"Got it," she said. "Any bottom line messages?"

"Yes," he said. "People care about butterflies, and I want them to care about sharks. But we've got a very, very small window to save them."

Standing, Sandra said, "All of that sounds perfect, so I think that's it. Since you folks want this to be part of the November MOI celebration, I'll have to get cracking on publicity. A talk about shark conservation is perfect for an invitation-only event for donors, reporters, and such. I'm pretty excited about the idea and will get you my promo draft in a couple of days."

After the publicist had thanked everyone and left, Harvey asked, "So is this a go?"

Brady nodded. "Yeah, I think so. We'll have to see what she writes, of course, but Sandra seems pretty sharp."

Saying, "Department business beckons," Harvey left us to work out details.

"One thing I'm wondering," I said, "is how a talk for donors and the press will be different from the one you already gave to MOI scientists."

Brady nodded. "Right. I need to work on that and would love your help. But in general there'd be less shark research and more about conservation, plus what amazing animals they are."

"You know," I said, "Online there are some pretty stunning videos people have made from shark cage footage. Since we've experienced shark cage diving ourselves, you could use some of that material to get people up close and personal with great whites."

Brady grinned. "I could talk about what it's like to be in the cage with sharks swimming all around you. People could really see how graceful and beautiful they are. It's a great idea."

"Good," I said. "But I'd leave out the bologna bit."

56

I BECAME INCREASINGLY ANXIOUS AS THE NOVEMBER EVENT approached. Would reporters from out of state actually travel to Spruce Harbor to hear a talk about sharks? Would the topic appeal to the all-important big-money doors? Had Sandra managed a publicity blitz with such limited notice?

Brady, on the other hand, seemed completely laid back about the whole thing. When I asked him if he was at all nervous he just shrugged and changed the subject.

On the morning of the big event, I asked Brady what he was going to wear.

He tipped his head to the side and answered, "Wear?"

"You know, as in clothes," I said.

"I'm not sure, but nothing special. Reporters and donors don't expect a field scientist to dress up for anything. If I walk onto the stage in a white shirt and clean khakis they'll be impressed."

"I'm sure people will want to talk with you afterwards," I said, "but Dixon didn't say anything about that."

"There's another invitation-only event for a smaller group in something called the Carriage House?"

"Whoa," I said. "First class. It's about a ten-minute walk from the auditorium, so no transportation needed. It's the kind of place where the help walks around with trays of champagne and expensive nibbles."

I walked down the center isle of MOI's auditorium a half-hour early and settled into a front-row seat. I hadn't attended a lecture since Brady's first one, and so very much had happened since then—Ted's dreadful behavior and my response, Cary's horrible death, using a shark decoy to trap Sean, spending time with Brady and eventually marrying him, and cage diving off Ensenada. Just thinking about it all amazed me.

Frederick Dixon introduced Brady as a world-class shark researcher especially interested in great white shark behavior and conservation who used scuba for his research in waters off California and Mexico. Then Brady strode onto the stage, adjusted a microphone at the podium, thanked Dixon for the introduction and generous support at MOI, and began his presentation. His first words surprised me.

"I would like to dedicate this talk to Eugenie Clark, whom I had the honor of working with at the Mote Marine Laboratory in Florida, which she founded. Popularly known as the Shark Lady, Eugenie was an ichthyologist who pioneered research on shark behavior. She was the first to use scuba for this work, and I am proud to be known as one of her students."

Brady's talk included much I'd heard before including the gruesome ways people kill them, their value to humans, and that someone is more likely to be killed by a tornado, lightning, or even falling airplane parts than by a shark. His "odds are higher that you'll go to the hospital after handling Christmas ornaments" got quite a few laughs.

During the presentation I turned around a couple of times to gauge people's reactions. Most appeared to be either taking notes or studying information Brady had projected on the screen. An hour after he started, Brady answered a few questions, thanked everyone, and strode off the stage.

The Carriage House was already bustling by the time I got there. I accepted a glass of champagne from a guy doing an excellent imitation of a butler, scanned the crowd for Brady, and spotted him on the other side of the room surrounded by a gaggle of reporters and donors. Unsure what to do, I stood there sipping champagne and people-watched.

Someone called my name, and I looked up to see Brady waving at me. As I approached he said, "Folks, please step aside so I can introduce you to one of MOI's most outstanding ocean-ographers, whom I'm sure you'll want to talk to."

When I reached him, Brady put his arm around my shoulder, pulled me closer, and said, "Mara Tusconi has viewed Maine's stunning deep-sea coral gardens in a submarine, gone scuba-diving in the vast Sargasso Sea, and confronted international eel traffickers right here in Maine. And these are just a few of her adventures your readers will love. This is a pretty large group, so why don't half of you go to one side and speak with Mara while the other half talks to me? In fifteen minutes or so we can switch."

And so it was a result of Brady's quick thinking and gener-osity that my ocean going exploits were featured in magazines and newspapers all around New England.

The following day I walked up Spruce Mountain to reflect on all that had happened since Brady MacFarlane gave his first lecture about sharks in MOI's auditorium. In a matter of months, a lovely young woman died from a shark attack, Ted declared his love for another woman, Brady and I watched sharks from underwater cages in Mexico where we fell in love, and Connor had married us in Angelo's backyard. It was dizzying, extraordi-nary, and very hard to take in.

Finally, after years of hope and heartbreak, I had found the generous and loving soul mate of my dreams.